A Voltaire Triptych

A Voltaire Triptych

Micromegas, Plato's Dream, Candide

Voltaire

Foreword by
Adam Roberts

Edited by
Carrie Christopher

"To hold a pen is to be at war."
Voltaire

Contents

Foreword
Adam Roberts

François-Marie Arouet (1694–1778), universally known by his *nom de plume* 'Voltaire', was the most celebrated writer and thinker of his age: a playwright and novelist, a philosopher and satirist, famous for his sharp wit, advocate of freedom of speech, freedom of religion, and separation of church and state. He was also astonishingly prolific: he published some 2000 books (some of these were, to be fair, not long) and over 20,000 letters: something like fifteen million words across his life. His most enduring works were his *contes philosophiques*, 'philosophical tales', novellas exploring contemporary concerns and metaphysical question via deftly framed stories and lively exchanges between characters. The most famous of these is *Candide, or The Optimist* (1762), in which the 'candid', ingenuous and rather gullible main character, goes about the harsh world convinced by the philosophical maxim of Leibniz: that 'all is for the best in this, the best of all possible worlds.' Leibniz's argument was that since the world was made by God, and since God is all good, all wise, all knowing and omnipotent, he must have created the best possible world. Candide's experiences of suffering, slavery, mutilation, misery and poverty gradually disabuse him of this idea.

Famous though Candide remains, in some ways the earlier *Micromégas* (1752) has had just as major an impact, not least because it is one of the earliest examples of science fiction. Ostensibly, it is the story of a gigantic alien being who travels from him home planet circling the star Sirius to tour the Galaxy. Arriving in our solar system, Micromégas befriends an inhabitant of the planet Saturn, also gigantic but not on the same scale as himself: Micromégas is '120,000 royal feet' tall, which is about 24 miles high: the Saturnian is a 'dwarf' by comparison, a mere 6,000 royal feet or 1.2 miles tall. The two travel on together, eventually coming to Earth, whose inhabitants—us—seem to them mere microbes. They study our world for a while, giving Voltaire the opportunity to satirise our self-importance and pomposity, for after all we are in the larger scheme of things tiny; and aiming some darts at human science, religious belief, and war-making.

The story works as a science-fictional fable: a 'peripatetic' (that is, moving from place to place) narrative and some amusing and charming observations. The sheer size of its title character, and the vast distances he has come, touch on what later science-fiction fans call the 'sense of wonder' that the genre is capable of generating. The whole story has a great deal of charm and point.

Some of that point, however, is lost to modern readerships. In the case of *Candide*, the fact that Leibniz remains a well-known philosophical name means that the satire of that novella continues to bite. *Micromégas* is also a satirical engagement with one of the great thinkers of the age of Voltaire, but his identity no longer has any wider currency, which means that readers of this witty, inventive space-fable can miss some of its force, and many of its gags.

Take, for example, the fact that Voltaire describes Mars as having two moons. What's remarkable is that these moons, Phobos and Deimos, were not discovered by American astronomer Asaph Hall, until 1877. Nonetheless, long before that discovery, Voltaire describes Micromégas passing the Red Planet on his way to Earth noticing them:

En sortant de Jupiter, ils traversèrent un espace d'environ cent millions de lieues, et ils côtoyèrent la planète de Mars, qui, comme on sait, est cinq fois plus petite que notre petit globe; ils virent deux lunes qui servent à cette planète, et qui ont échappé aux regards de nos astronomes. Je sais bien que le père Castel écrira, et même assez plaisamment, contre l'existence de ces deux lunes; mais je m'en rapporte à ceux qui raisonnent par analogie. Ces bons philosophes-là savent combien il serait difficile que Mars, qui est si loin du soleil, se passât à moins de deux lunes.

When they took leave of Jupiter, they traversed a space of about one hundred million leagues, and coasting along the planet Mars, which is well known to be five times smaller than our little earth, they descried two moons subservient to that orb which have escaped the observation of all our astronomers. I know Father Castel will write, and that pleasantly enough, against the existence of these two moons; but I entirely refer myself to those who reason by analogy. Those worthy philosophers are very sensible that Mars, which is at such a distance from the sun, must be in a very uncomfortable situation, without the benefit of a couple of moons.

How did Voltaire know that Mars had two moons, 125 years before they were first observed?

The answer is: Fontenelle. The remarkably long-lived Bernard Le Bovier de Fontenelle (he died in 1757, a mere month before his hundredth birthday) was a major figure of French 17th- and 18th-century science, perpetual secretary of the Académie des Sciences in Paris, author of all sorts of books on all manner of topics. A generation older than Voltaire, he published some of his most famous works before the later author was even born, among them: *Nouveaux dialogues des morts* ('New dialogues on death', 1683), *De l'origine des fables* ('The origin of legends', 1684), *Histoire des oracles* ('History of oracles', 1687), *Digression sur les anciens et les modernes* ('Dissertation on the ancients and moderns', 1688) and perhaps his most famous work, *Entretiens sur la pluralité des mondes* ('Discussion concerning the plurality of worlds', 1686; revised 1724). Part of this latter work was a speculation about the function of moons as such. Why is it, Fontenelle asks, that Mercury and Venus have no moons, Earth one, and Jupiter and Saturn many? It must be—or so he reasons—that God, or Providence, furnishes these moons to light up what would otherwise be a lightless night sky, for the benefit of the inhabitants of these worlds. The further away from the sun, the fainter sunlight, the darker the night, and therefore the more moons are needful for this task. But wait! 'Mais attendez; il me semble que Mars, qui est encore plus éloigné du soleil que la terre, n'a point de lune,' says Fontanelle ('But wait: it strikes me that Mars, further away from the sun than Earth, doesn't have a moon'). How can this be? Fontenelle speculates that perhaps Martian rocks are luminous, absorbing sunlight during the day and releasing it at night ('Peut-être Mars a-t-il de grands rochers fort élevés, qui sont des phosphores naturels, et qui prennent pendant le jour une provision de lumière qu'ils rendent pendant la nuit') but he inclines towards a simpler solution: Mars *does* have moons, it's just that we haven't yet seen them. And if it does have moons, it must, being further from the sun, have more moons than Earth.

That Voltaire was engaging with Fontenelle in *Micromégas*

isn't news. It's long been known that the mile-high-man from Saturn whom Micromégas first meets when he comes to our solar system, the 'secretary of the Saturnian scientific society' is a caricature of Fontenelle. Our Saturnian 'dwarf'—a disparaging kind of name, until we remember that he's only a dwarf when compared to the 24-mile-high Micromégas—is a scientist. When he does come to Earth, he observes the 'intelligent atoms' that inhabit that tiny world through a microscope. At one point he thinks he sees humans having sex:

> *The Saturnian, passing from an excess of incredulity to an excess of credulity, thought he saw them mating. "Ah" he said. "I have caught nature in the act." But he was fooled by appearances, which happens only too often, whether one is using a microscope or not.*

The French phrase here is: *j'ai pris la nature sur le fait*, a comic double-entendre that means both 'I have observed the workings of nature' and also 'I have seen nature fucking'. It's based on a passage from Fontenelle's eulogy for Joseph Pitton de Tournefort [*Éloge de Tournefort* (1708), 54 55]. Botanist Tournefort had travelled around the Mediterranean and the near East, making a series of observations and discoveries:

> *Tournefort eut la sensible joie d'y voir une nouvelle espèce de jardin, dont toutes les plantes étaient différentes pièces de marbre encore naissantes ou jeunes ... En vain la nature s'était cachée dans des lieux si profonds et si inaccessibles pour travailler à la végétation des pierres; elle fut, pour ainsi dire, prise sur le fait par des curieux si hardis.*
>
> *Tournefort had the particular joy of discovering in those places a wholly new kind of garden, all the plants of which were growing in various crenulations and crevices of marble ...*

Adam Roberts

*In vain had nature hidden herself in places so deep and so
inaccessible to work on the vegetation of the stones; she was, so
to speak, caught in the act by such bold onlookers.*

People laughed, here, at Fontenelle's inadvertent double-
entendre, and Voltaire mockingly stuck it into *Micromégas*.

Ira Wade thinks the extent to which *Micromégas* is all
about making fun of Fontenelle can be overstated: It is possible
to exaggerate the role played by Fontenelle in the Micromégas.
It is true that the flowery language of the Secretary of the
Academy of Saturn suggests Fontenelle's much criticized style.
The expression *J'ai pris la nature sur le fait* was a witticism
connected with Fontenelle. All in all, however, Voltaire's barbs
at Fontenelle are not particularly severe. They indicate not so
much a decided antagonism, or a deep animosity, but rather a
passing irritation.[1]

As Wade notes, 'Fontenelle was Secretary of the Academy
of Sciences, and Voltaire at the time had ambitions in that
direction' which Fontenelle did not facilitate, although the
specific focus of irritation was, it seems clear, Fontenelle's
comment upon reading Voltaire's *Eléments de la philosophie de
Newton* ('Elements of Newton's Philosophy' 1738). He is
supposed to have said, 'very good, Monsieur Voltaire: another
three years of study, and perhaps you will actually begin to
understand Newton.' Ouch!

So: Micromégas is a 25-mile-high giant from the star Sirius,
who flies easily around the galaxy examining all he finds with
scientific passion and disinterest, making all manner of brilliant
discoveries. His Saturnian companion is, by comparison, a
dwarf, a significant figure in his own right, but by comparison

------

1. Ira Wade, *Voltaire's Micromégas: a Study in the Fusion of Science, Myth
and Art* (Princeton University Press, 1950), 24

with the illustrious Micromégas a nobody, a pigmy. If the Saturnian is Fontenelle, then who is Micromégas himself?

The novella does not spell this out, but surely the answer is: Newton. Just as *Candide* is a novel spun out of Voltaire's engagement with Leibniz, so Micromégas is novel that renders Newton's magnitude into a science-fiction fable. How does our hero travel? Like Newton, 'il connaissait merveilleusement les lois de la gravitation, et toutes les forces attractives et répulsives' ('he had a marvellous understanding of the laws of gravity and all attractive-repulsive forces').

> *Il s'en servait si à propos, que, tantôt à l'aide d'un rayon du soleil, tantôt par la commodité d'une comète, il allait de globe en globe lui et les siens, comme un oiseau voltige de branche en branche.*
>
> *He made use of it so aptly that, now with the aid of a ray of starlight, now by the convenience of a comet, he went from planet to planet, he and those like him, like a bird fluttering from branch to branch.*

Why, then, Sirius? And why Saturn? Because, in one of his more famous experiments, Newton in the 1670s measured the relative brightness of precisely those two bodies, with a view to establishing their relative distances from Earth via the inverse square law. In observing the night sky, Newton noted that Sirius was about as bright as the planet Saturn. Observations of Mars by John Flamsteed in 1672 had established that Saturn is about nine- to ten-times farther from the Sun than Earth, so Newton could use that to determine the distance to Sirius. Sirius and Saturn appeared equally bright, but Sirius was much farther away. The catch was that Sirius, being a star, emits its own light like the Sun, but Saturn shines by reflecting sunlight. So Newton had to calculate how much sunlight would reach

Saturn. This is pretty easy to do with the inverse-square law, but Saturn also doesn't reflect all of the light that strikes it, so Newton had to estimate the fraction of light the planet reflects (known as its albedo). In the end, Newton calculated that Sirius was about 800,000 times the distance of Earth from the Sun, or about 12.6 light years. The actual distance is about 8.6 light years, so Newton was at least in the ballpark (his biggest mistake was greatly underestimating the albedo of Saturn, but he also assumed Sirius was the same brightness as the Sun, when it is actually much brighter).

Whatever beef he had with Fontenelle, Voltaire had the highest opinion of Newton. In the words of Julia Epstein, 'Voltaire's portrait of Newton in the Lettres philosophiques and in his *Elemens de la philosophie de Newton* presents one of the most dynamic images of the scientist as a hero and as a creative imagination. In 1732, Voltaire wrote to Maupertuis: "[Newton] est notre Christophe Colomb. Il nous a menez dans un nouveau monde, et je voudrois bien y voiager..."[2] Elsewhere he called Newton "le dieu au quel je sacrifie" and "l'esprit créateur" ('the god to whom I sacrifice' and 'the creator-spirit'). (It's from Voltaire, incidentally, that we get the apocryphal story of Newton 'discovering' gravity when an apple falls in his head—in fact, the apple-on-the-head almost certainly never happened). Newton is *micro-* because he was, in himself, physically small (as a child his mother used to say he was tiny enough to fit inside a quart pot), but *-megas* because he was a giant of science. Newton is Micromégas.

An even greater name than Newton is Greek philosopher Plato, the subject of 'Plato's Dream' (written early in Voltaire's life, probably in 1737, but not published until 1754). This short piece takes its place in a venerable tradition of 'Dream'

---

2. Epstein, 'Voltaire's Myth of Newton', *Pacific Coast Philology*, 14 (1979), 27

works in which, under the conceit of a character falling asleep and dreaming, a cosmic voyage can be related. The Roman politician and writer Cicero wrote the *Somnium Scipionis*, 'The Dream of Scipio', in the late 50s BC: it relates the voyage of the famous Roman general Scipio Aemilianus through the solar system. Renaissance astronomer Johannes Kepler wrote his *Somnium* sometime in the early AD 1600s (it was published after his death, in 1632): in this short book a character dreams of flying to the moon, and observing the strange alien life-forms that exist there. Voltaire's contribution to this small genre is more sardonic: his Plato dreams of Démiourgos, 'the Demiurge' the Latinised form of the Greek δημιουργός, a being described in Plato's *Timaeus* (c. 360 BC) as the creator of the universe: the Greek word originally meant 'craftsman' or 'maker'. Beneath this creator-God Voltaire imagines less capable entities called 'genii', amongst them one Démogorgon who is tasked with creating Earth. He does this and is pleased with his result, until his fellow genii criticise what he has done.

Vraiment vous avez fort bien opéré: vous avez séparé votre monde en deux, et vous avez mis un grand espace d'eau entre les deux hémisphères, afin qu'il n'y eût point de communication de l'un à l'autre. On gèlera de froid sous vos deux pôles, on mourra de chaud sous votre ligne équinoxiale ... Vos oignons et vos artichauts sont de très-bonnes choses, mais je ne vois pas quelle a été votre idée en couvrant la terre de tant de plantes venimeuses, à moins que vous n'ayez eu le dessin d'empoisonner ses habitants. Il me paraît d'ailleurs que vous avez formé une trentaine d'espèces de singes, beaucoup plus d'espèces de chiens, et seulement quatre ou cinq espèces d'hommes: il est vrai que vous avez donné à ce dernier animal ce que vous appelez la raison; mais, en conscience, cette raison-là est trop ridicule, et approche trop de la folie.

Truly you have performed mighty feats! You have divided your world into two parts; and, to prevent them from communicating with each other, placed a vast collection of waters between the two hemispheres. The inhabitants must perish with cold under both your poles, and be scorched to death under the equator ... Your onions and artichokes are very good things, but I cannot conceive what induced you to scatter such a heap of poisonous plants over the face of the planet, unless it was to poison its inhabitants. Moreover, if I am not mistaken, you have created about 30 different kinds of monkeys, a still greater number of dogs, yet only four or five races of humans. It is true, indeed, you have bestowed on the latter of these animals a faculty you call Reason, but it is so poorly executed that you might better call it Folly.

Stung, Démogorgon insists the other genii examine the shortcomings of the work of the other genii: Jupiter and Saturn, similarly mixtures of good and bad. The story ends when the Demiurge himself intervenes, rebukes his underlings and tells them they are themselves imperfect and so can only produce mixed, imperfect creations.

Of *Candide*, one of the most famous European novels ever written, there is little to say that hasn't been said before. Its ingenuous, cheerful hero, whose name means both candid and white (from the Latin *candidus*) travels widely, encountering, among other things, massacre, pillage, rape, piracy, mutilation, brutal militarism, cannibalism, slavery, bestiality, vivisection, religious fanaticism and political intolerance. So grim a set of events could be depressing or revolting, but Voltaire writes the whole with a deft satirical buoyancy, a piercing lightness of tone, sharp wit, dazzling observation. At the same time, it is worth noting how profound are the philosophical questions the novel addresses: for this is a conte philosophique, a 'philosophical tale'. In the words of the great Jacob Bronowski: 'in a supposedly harmonious and lawful universe, how do we explain the existence of evil?' It is difficult to think of a more serious and important question than this one, and it is Voltaire's genius that he addresses it, genuinely and with real insight and wisdom, in the mode of comedy. However brutal and distressing Candide's adventures are, the tone of the novel manages to maintain a funny, ironic good-humour throughout. That one can talk about serious matters via comedy and laughter is, in its way, an insight worthy of the description profound. Of the original question, Bronowski says:

> *On this profound question of theodicy Voltaire found himself in opposition to the facile optimism of men like Leibnitz. Against the view that 'all is for the best in this the best of all possible worlds', Voltaire placed the 'real' world of his hero, Candide. The book is too famous to need paraphrasing. It is enough to say that wandering from Westphalia, through Paraguay and El Dorado, and finally ending in Turkey, Candide experienced disasters almost all the way. Candide is a magnificent satire in the form of a travel story.*[3]

Voltaire puts into the mouth of Pangloss, Candide's buffoonish tutor, a—we must be honest—simplified and rather distorted version of Leibniz's view of the inevitable beneficence of our God-created world. In his *Théodicée* (1710) Leibniz does not deny that aspects of our existence involve suffering and even evil; but it does say that we cannot judge whether these things are disproportionate, or unnecessary, until we have the 'whole sight' of God at the end of time. Voltaire takes a simpli-

---

3. Jacob Bronowski, with Bruce Mazlish, *The Western Intellectual Tradition: from Leonardo to Hegel* (Harmondsworth: Penguin 1963), 295

fied version of Leibniz's optimism, and sets it in the context of his recent history. The Seven Years War (1756-1763) involved not only massive casualties on the battlefield (something like 800,000 soldiers died in the course of the conflict) but huge distress, displacement and death among the civilian populations of Europe, including theft from, and murder and rape of, non-combatants on a hideous scale. Also on Voltaire's mind was the terrible earthquake that struck the Portuguese city of Lisbon on November 1, 1755, shattering the town to pieces and killing many: of the city's 200,000 inhabitants, perhaps a fifth— 40,000 people—were killed (tens of thousands more died along the coasts of Portugal and Morocco). It was a staggering natural disaster, and the fact that it happened on All Saints Day struck many as bitterly ironic. Voltaire takes these events, war, human rapine and cruelty, natural disaster, as the default of our world, and sends Candide and his friends on a pilgrimage of suffering through it all.

The suffering is, as Erich Auerbach observed, excessive, but deliberately so, a succession of increasingly horrible things described with a 'rapidity, an alertness, of tempo' enables 'a giddy, swift, high-spirited narrative in which black and white, theory and practice, etc., are set in clear and simple opposition.' The rhythm of the adventures which befall Candide and his companions is to be nowhere observed in the reality of experience. Such a relentless, unrelated torrent of mishaps pouring down from a clear sky on the heads of perfectly innocent and unprepared people whom it involves by mere chance, simply does not exist. It is much more like the mishaps of a comic figure in a farce or a clown in a circus.[4]

This is exactly the point: the sheer quantity of 'mishaps'

---

4. Erich Auerbach, *Mimesis: the Presentation of Reality in Western Literature* (New York Doubleday 1957), 360

afflicting Candide and his companions freights the novel by their persistence as dark comedy. The world, Voltaire is saying, is saturated with suffering. To look at human existence and say, as Leibniz appeared to do, that it was not possible to imagine it better is, simply, a joke.

But *Candide* would not be as great a novel as it is if all it did was tear down Leibniz's facile optimism. It does more than this. It puts in place an alternative philosophy of life. With deceptive simplicity Voltaire puts into Candide's mouth a piece of brilliant practical philosophy:

> *Cela est bien dit, rèpondit Candide, mais il faut cultiver notre jardin."*
>
> "All that is very well," answered Candide, "but let us cultivate our garden."

Candide is literally working in his garden, finding peace and contentment at last. But these words have a wider application than horticulture. For all of us, happiness means: finding something productive and useful, something local and to hand, and working at it. *Cultiver*, 'to cultivate', means literally to work a garden or plot of land, but it also means to elevate a human being into the higher, more cultured, existence—*culture* comes from the same etymological root—and so glances at the arts and humanities, the customs and lifestyles that enrich and magnify bare human existence. We should all work towards these things, Voltaire is saying. After so much suffering and endurance, it is a profoundly hopeful conclusion.

Voltaire himself put it into practice. Whilst writing Candide, whilst living in Switzerland, he got into trouble with the Swiss government, because of his free-thinking writing. He moved to an estate on the Swiss-French border, Ferney, choosing the location so that he could slip into France if the

Swiss authorities turned up to arrest him. When he bought the place it was a small settlement, and more or less a wilderness. He 'cultivated this garden' by draining marshes, bringing unused land under the plough, planting vines and fruit trees, creating a stud farm and setting-up industries on the estate, including silk weaving and pocket-watch manufacture. In the words of Thomas Walsh:

> 'in an idyllic setting which commanded views over Mont Blanc, Voltaire henceforward devoted his life to his own and his tenants' well-being, abolishing feudal dues, stimulated the local economy, welcomed industrious political refugees, staged festivals, parties and theatrical events and rebuilt the parish church... Voltaire's ideas of cooperation among people and the value of working to avoid boredom and vice helped to transform a small community of fewer than one hundred people into a thriving small city of over twelve hundred. There was work for all, and Voltaire mandated fair practices in conducting business and governmental affairs. Voltaire was in his ideal world. As patron of the town, he lived out his own philosophies.'[5]

Adam Roberts
Head of Department
Professor of 19th-century Literature, English
Royal Holloway, University of London

---

5. Thomas Walsh, *Readings in* Candide (San Diego, CA: Greenhaven Press 2001), 21

Editor's Note
Carrie Christopher

I chose to re-issue these three Voltaire classics based on my love of author Neal Stephensen's *Quicksilver Trilogy*, set mostly in the period when Voltaire was alive and chafing against the confines of church, state, and intellectual discourse.

Through the course of editing these works, I had the fortune to work with foreword author Adam Roberts, a Voltaire scholar with serious science fiction and fantasy writing chops (read *Salt*, it's amazing). Adam's theories of the men lampooned in *Micromégas*, along with his direct translations of some passages, bring Voltaire's work to life.

I'm grateful for Adam's contributions to *A Voltaire Triptych*. Like Kevin J. Anderson, Adam Roberts is a ridiculously prolific writer and scholar. I encourage you to read his books.

Re-issuing classics that are a few hundred years old bring unique challenges. The English language evolves, and the grammar, punctuation, and especially those darned compound adjectives have been preserved the stay true to the language of that time.

I thought long and hard about some of the wording and scenes that reflected the Western cultural biases of Voltaire's time. I considered alternate word choices and omissions for a handful of words and sentences in the triptych. After intensive debate and discussion, it was decided to leave the language intact for historical accuracy and respect for Voltaire's body of work.

These are great stories full of absurdity, satire, and wit. I loved diving deep into Voltaire's mind and imagination, and see many themes still ringing true, even today. I hope you enjoy *A Voltaire Triptych*.

Let us cultivate our gardens.

Carrie Christopher
Editor, *A Voltaire Triptych*,
and author, artist, publisher,
Carrie Christopher Creative LLC

Micromegas

A VOYAGE TO THE PLANET SATURN BY A NATIVE OF SIRIUS

In one of the planets that revolve round the star known by the name of Sirius was a certain young gentleman of promising parts, whom I had the honor to be acquainted with in his last voyage to this our little ant-hill. His name was Micromégas, an appellation suited to all great men, and his stature amounted to eight leagues in height, that is, twenty-four thousand geometrical paces of five feet each.

Some of your mathematicians, a set of people always useful to the public, will perhaps instantly seize the pen and calculate that Mr. Micromégas, inhabitant of the country of Sirius, being from head to foot four and twenty thousand paces in length, making one hundred and twenty thousand royal feet, that we, denizens of this earth, being at a medium little more than five feet high, and our globe nine thousand leagues in circumference; these things being premised, they will then conclude that the periphery of the globe which produced him must be exactly one and twenty millions six hundred thousand times greater than that of this, our tiny ball.

Nothing in nature is more simple and common. The

dominions of some sovereigns of Germany or Italy, which may be compassed in half an hour, when compared with the Ottoman, Russian, or Chinese empires, are no other than faint instances of the prodigious difference that nature has made in the scale of beings. The stature of his excellency being of these extraordinary dimensions, all our artists will agree that the measure around his body might amount to fifty thousand royal feet, a very agreeable and just proportion.

His nose being equal in length to one-third of his face, and his jolly countenance engrossing one-seventh part of his height, it must be owned that the nose of this same Sirian was six thousand three hundred and thirty-three royal feet, to a hair, which was to be demonstrated. With regard to his understanding, it is one of the best cultivated I have known. He is perfectly well acquainted with abundance of things, some of which are of his own invention; for, when his age did not exceed two hundred and fifty years, he studied according to the custom of the country, at the most celebrated university of the whole planet, and by the force of his genius discovered upwards of fifty propositions of Euclid, having the advantage by more than eighteen of Blaise Pascal, who (as we are told by his own sister), demonstrated two and thirty for his amusement and then left off, choosing rather to be an indifferent philosopher than a great mathematician.

About the four hundred and fiftieth year of his age, or latter end of his childhood, he dissected a great number of small insects not more than one hundred feet in diameter, which are not perceivable by ordinary microscopes, on which he composed a very curious treatise, which involved him in some trouble. The mufti of the nation, though very old and very ignorant, made shift to discover in his book certain lemmas that were suspicious, unseemly, rash, heretic, and unsound, and prosecuted him with great animosity; for the subject of the author's inquiry was whether, in the world of Sirius, there was any difference between the substantial forms of a flea and a snail.

Micromégas defended his philosophy with such spirit as made all the female sex his proselytes; and the process lasted two hundred and twenty years; at the end of which time, in consequence of the mufti's interest, the book was condemned by judges who had never read it, and the author expelled from court for the term of eight hundred years.

Not much affected at his banishment from a court that teemed with nothing but turmoils and trifles, he made a very humorous song upon the mufti, who gave himself no trouble about the matter, and set out on his travels from planet to planet in order (as the saying is) to improve his mind and finish his education. Those who never travel but in a post-chaise or berlin, will doubtless be astonished at the equipages used above, for we that strut upon this little molehill are at a loss to conceive anything that surpasses our own customs. But our traveler was a wonderful adept in the laws of gravitation, together with the whole force of attraction and repulsion, and made such seasonable use of his knowledge that sometimes by the help of a sunbeam, and sometimes by the convenience of a comet, he and his retinue glided from sphere to sphere, as the bird hops from one bough to another.

He in a very little time posted through the Milky Way, and I am obliged to own he saw not a twinkle of those stars supposed to adorn that fair empyrean which the illustrious Dr. Derham brags to have observed through his telescope. Not that I pretend to say the doctor was mistaken. God forbid! But Micromégas was upon the spot, an exceedingly good observer, and I have no mind to contradict any man.

Be that as it may, after many windings and turnings, he arrived at the planet Saturn, and, accustomed as he was to the sight of novelties, he could not for his life repress a supercilious and conceited smile, which often escapes the wisest philosopher, when he perceived the smallness of that globe and the diminutive size of its inhabitants; for really Saturn is but about nine hundred times larger than this our earth, and the people of that country mere dwarfs, about a thousand fathoms high.

In short, he at first derided those poor pygmies, just as an Indian fiddler laughs at the music of Lully, at his first arrival in Paris; but as this Sirian was a person of good sense, he soon perceived that a thinking being may not be altogether ridiculous, even though he is not quite six thousand feet high; and therefore he became familiar with them, after they had ceased to wonder at his extraordinary appearance. In particular, he contracted an intimate friendship with the secretary of the Academy of Saturn, a man of good understanding, who, though in truth he had invented nothing of his own, gave a very good account of the inventions of others, and enjoyed in peace the reputation of a little poet and great calculator. And here, for the edification of the reader, I will repeat a very singular conversation that one day passed between Mr. Secretary and Micromégas.

THE CONVERSATION BETWEEN MICROMEGAS AND THE INHABITANT OF SATURN

His excellency having laid himself down, and the secretary approached his nose:

"It must be confessed," said Micromegas, "that nature is full of variety."

"Yes," replied the Saturnian, "nature is like a parterre, whose flowers—"

"Pshaw!" cried the other, "a truce with your parterres."

"It is," resumed the secretary, "like an assembly of fair and brown women, whose dresses—"

"What a plague have I to do with your brunettes?" said our traveler.

"Then it is like a gallery of pictures, the strokes of which—"

"Not at all," answered Micromegas, "I tell you, once and for all, nature is like nature, and comparisons are odious."

"Well, to please you," said the secretary.

"I won't be pleased," replied the Sirian, "I want to be instructed; begin, therefore, without further preamble, and tell me how many senses the people of this world enjoy."

"We have seventy and two," said the academician, "but we

are daily complaining of the small number, as our imagination transcends our wants, for, with the seventy-two senses, our five moons and ring, we find ourselves very much restricted; and notwithstanding our curiosity, and the no small number of those passions that result from these few senses, we have still time enough to be tired of idleness."

"I sincerely believe what you say," cried Micromegas, "for, though we Sirians have near a thousand different senses, there still remains a certain vague desire, an unaccountable inquietude incessantly admonishing us of our own unimportance, and giving us to understand that there are other beings who are much our superiors in point of perfection. I have travelled a little, and seen mortals both above and below myself in the scale of being, but I have met with none who had not more desire than necessity, and more want than gratification. Perhaps I shall one day arrive in some country where naught is wanting, but hitherto I have had no certain information of such a happy land."

The Saturnian and his guest exhausted themselves in conjectures upon this subject, and after an abundance of argumentation equally ingenious and uncertain, were fain to return to matter of fact.

"To what age do you commonly live?" said the Sirian.

"Lackaday! A mere trifle," replied the little gentleman.

"It is the very same case with us," resumed the other, "the shortness of life is our daily complaint, so that this must be a universal law in nature."

"Alas!" cried the Saturnian, "few, very few on this globe outlive five hundred great revolutions of the sun (these, according to our way of reckoning, amount to about fifteen thousand years). So, you see, we in a manner begin to die the very moment we are born; our existence is no more than a point, our duration an instant, and our globe an atom. Scarce do we begin to learn a little, when death intervenes before we can profit by experience. For my own part, I am deterred from laying schemes when I consider myself as a single drop in the midst of an immense ocean. I am particularly ashamed, in your presence, of the ridiculous figure I make among my fellow-creatures."

To this declaration Micromegas replied, "If you were not a philosopher, I should be afraid of mortifying your pride by telling you that the term of our lives is seven hundred times longer than the length of your existence; but you are very sensible that when the texture of the body is resolved, in order to reanimate nature in another form, which is the consequence of what we call death—when that moment of change arrives, there is not the least difference betwixt having lived a whole eternity or a single day. I have been in some countries where the people live a thousand times longer than us, and yet they murmured at the shortness of their time. But one will find everywhere some few persons of good sense, who know how to make the best of their portion and thank the author of nature for its bounty. There is a profusion of variety scattered through the universe, and yet there is an admirable vein of uniformity that runs through the whole; for example, all thinking beings are different among themselves, though at bottom they resemble one another in the powers and passions of the soul. Matter, though interminable, hath different properties in every sphere. How many principal attributes do you reckon in the matter of this world?"

"If you mean those properties," said the Saturnian, "without which we believe this our globe could not subsist, we reckon in all three hundred, such as extent, impenetrability, motion, gravitation, divisibility, etcetera. "

"That small number," replied the traveler, "probably answers the views of the Creator on this your narrow sphere. I adore its wisdom in all its works. I see infinite variety, but everywhere proportion. Your globe is small, so are the inhabitants. You have few sensations, because your matter is endued with few properties. These are the works of unerring providence. Of what color does your sun appear when accurately examined?"

"Of a yellowish white," answered the Saturnian, "and in separating one of his rays we find it contains seven colors."

"Our sun," said the Sirian, "is of a reddish hue, and we have no less than thirty-nine original colors. Among all the suns I have seen there is no sort of resemblance, and in this sphere of yours there is not one face like another."

After diverse questions of this nature he asked how many substances, essentially different, they counted in the world of Saturn, and understood that they numbered but thirty, such as God, space, matter, beings endowed with sense and extension, beings that have extension, sense, and reflection; thinking beings who have no extension; those that are penetrable; those that are impenetrable, and also all others. But this Saturnian philosopher was prodigiously astonished when the Sirian told him they had no less than three hundred, and that he himself had discovered three thousand more in the course of his travels. In short, after having communicated to each other what they knew, and even what they did not know, and argued during a complete revolution of the sun, they resolved to set out together on a small philosophical tour.

THE VOYAGE OF
THESE INHABITANTS
OF OTHER WORLDS

Our two philosophers were just ready to embark from the atmosphere of Saturn, with a large provision of mathematical instruments, when the Saturnian's mistress, having got an inkling of their design, came all in tears to make her protests. She was a handsome brunette, though not above six hundred and threescore fathoms high; but her agreeable attractions made amends for the smallness of her stature.

"Ah! cruel man," cried she, "after a courtship of fifteen hundred years, when at length I surrendered and became your wife, and scarce have passed two hundred more in thy embraces, to leave me thus, before the honeymoon is over, and go a-rambling with a giant of another world! Go, go, thou art a mere virtuoso, devoid of tenderness and love! If thou wert a true Saturnian, thou wouldst be faithful and invariable. Ah! Whither art thou going? What is thy design? Our five moons are not so inconstant, nor our ring so changeable as thee! But take this along with thee, henceforth I ne'er shall love another man."

The little gentleman embraced and wept over her, notwithstanding his philosophy; and the lady, after having swooned with great decency, went to console herself with more agreeable company.

Meanwhile our two virtuosi set out, and at one jump leaped upon the ring, which they found pretty flat, according to the ingenious guess of an illustrious inhabitant of this our little earth. From thence they easily slipped from moon to moon; and a comet chancing to pass, they sprang upon it with all their servants and apparatus. Thus carried about one hundred and fifty millions of leagues, they met with the satellites of Jupiter, and arrived upon the body of the planet itself, where they continued a whole year; during which they learned some very curious secrets, which would actually be sent to the press, were it not for fear of the gentlemen inquisitors, who have found among them some corollaries very hard of digestion.

Nevertheless, I have read the manuscript in the library of the illustrious archbishop, who, with that generosity and goodness which should ever be commended, has granted me permission to peruse his books; wherefore I promise he shall have a long article in the next edition of Moréri, and I shall not forget the young gentlemen, his sons, who give us such pleasing hopes of seeing perpetuated the race of their illustrious father.

But to return to our travelers. When they took leave of Jupiter, they traversed a space of about one hundred million leagues, and coasting along the planet Mars, which is well known to be five times smaller than our little earth, they descried two moons subservient to that orb which have escaped the observation of all our astronomers. I know Father Castel will write, and that pleasantly enough, against the existence of these two moons; but I entirely refer myself to those who reason by analogy. Those worthy philosophers are very sensible that Mars, which is at such a distance from the sun, must be in a very uncomfortable situation, without the benefit of a couple of moons.

Be that as it may, our gentlemen found the planet so small that they were afraid they should not find room to take a little repose, so that they pursued their journey like two travelers who despise the paltry accommodation of a village and push forward to the next market town. But the Sirian and his companion soon repented of their delicacy, for they journeyed a long time without finding a resting-place, till at length they discerned a small speck, which was the Earth. Coming from Jupiter, they could not but be moved with compassion at the sight of this miserable spot, upon which, however, they resolved to land, lest they should be a second time disappointed. They accordingly moved toward the tail of the comet, where, finding an aurora borealis ready to set sail, they embarked, and arrived on the northern coast of the Baltic on the fifth day of July, new style, in the year 1737.

WHAT BEFELL THEM
UPON THIS OUR GLOBE

Having taken some repose, and being desirous of reconnoitering the narrow field in which they were, they traversed it at once from north to south. Every step of the Sirian and his attendants measured about thirty thousand royal feet, whereas the dwarf of Saturn, whose stature did not exceed a thousand fathoms, followed at a distance quite out of breath; because, for every single stride of his companion, he was obliged to make twelve good steps at least. The reader may figure to themself (if we are allowed to make such comparisons) a very little rough spaniel dodging after a captain of the Prussian grenadiers.

As those strangers walked at a good pace, they compassed the globe in six and thirty hours; the sun, it is true, or rather the earth, describes the same space in the course of one day; but it must be observed that it is much easier to turn upon an axis than to walk afoot. Behold them then returned to the spot from whence they had set out, after having discovered that almost imperceptible sea, which is called the Mediterranean, and the other narrow pond that surrounds this mole-hill, under the denomination of the great ocean, in wading through which the dwarf had never wet his mid-leg, while the other scarce moistened his heel. In going and coming through both hemispheres, they did all that lay in their power to discover whether or not the globe was inhabited. They stooped, they lay down, they groped in every corner; but their eyes and hands were not at all proportioned to the small beings that crawl upon this earth, and, therefore, they could not find the smallest reason to suspect that we and our fellow-citizens of this globe had the honor to exist.

The dwarf, who sometimes judged too hastily, concluded at once that there were no living creatures upon earth, and his chief reason was that he had seen nobody. But Micromegas, in a polite manner, made him sensible of the unjust conclusion:

"For," said he, "with your diminutive eyes you cannot see certain stars of the fiftieth magnitude, which I easily perceive. "Do you take it for granted that no such stars exist?"

"But I have groped with great care." replied the dwarf.

"Then your sense of feeling must be bad." said the other.

"But this globe," said the dwarf, "is ill-contrived, and so irregular in its form as to be quite ridiculous. The whole together looks like chaos. Do but observe these little rivulets; not one of them runs in a straight line; and these ponds which are neither round, square, nor oval, nor indeed of any regular figure; together with these little sharp pebbles (meaning the mountains) that roughen the whole surface of the globe, and have torn all the skin from my feet. Besides, pray take notice of the shape of the whole, how it flattens at the poles, and turns round the sun in an awkward oblique manner, so that the polar circles cannot possibly be cultivated. Truly, what makes me believe there is no inhabitant on this sphere is a full persuasion that no sensible being would live in such a disagreeable place."

"What then?" said Micromegas; "Perhaps the beings that

inhabit it come not under that denomination; but, to all appearance, it was not made for nothing. Everything here seems to you irregular, because you fetch all your comparisons from Jupiter or Saturn. Perhaps this is the very reason of the seeming confusion which you condemn; have I not told you that in the course of my travels I have always met with variety?"

The Saturnian replied to all these arguments, and perhaps the dispute would have known no end, if Micromegas, in the heat of the contest, had not luckily broken the string of his diamond necklace, so that the jewels fell to the ground; they consisted of pretty small unequal stones, the largest of which weighed four hundred pounds, and the smallest fifty. The dwarf, in helping to pick them up, perceived, as they approached his eye, that every single diamond was cut in such a manner as to answer the purpose of an excellent microscope. He therefore took up a small one, about one hundred and sixty feet in diameter, and applied it to his eye, while Micromegas chose another of two thousand five hundred feet. Though they were of excellent powers, the observers could perceive nothing by their assistance, so they were altered and adjusted.

At length, the inhabitant of Saturn discerned something almost imperceptible moving between two waves in the Baltic. This was no other than a whale, which, in a dexterous manner, he caught with his little finger, and, placing it on the nail of his thumb, showed it to the Sirian, who laughed heartily at the excessive smallness peculiar to the inhabitants of this our globe. The Saturnian, by this time convinced that our world was inhabited, began to imagine we had no other animals than whales; and being a mighty debater, he forthwith set about investigating the origin and motion of this small atom, curious to know whether or not it was furnished with ideas, judgment, and free will.

Micromegas was very much perplexed upon this subject.

He examined the animal with the most patient attention, and the result of his inquiry was that he could see no reason to believe a soul was lodged in such a body. The two travelers were actually inclined to think there was no such thing as mind in this our habitation, when, by the help of their microscope, they perceived something as large as a whale floating upon the surface of the sea. It is well known that at this period a flock of philosophers were upon their return from the polar circle, where they had been making observations, for which nobody has hitherto been the wiser. The gazettes record that their vessel ran ashore on the coast of Bothnia and that they with great difficulty saved their lives; but in this world one can never dive to the bottom of things.

For my own part, I will ingeniously recount the transaction just as it happened, without any addition of my own; and this is no small effort in a modern historian.

THE TRAVELLERS CAPTURE A SEA VESSEL

Micromegas stretched out his hand gently toward the place where the object appeared, and advanced two fingers, which he instantly pulled back, for fear of being disappointed; then opening softly and shutting them all at once, he very dexterously seized the ship that contained those gentlemen, and placed it on his nail, avoiding too much pressure, which might have crushed the whole in pieces.

"This," said the Saturnian dwarf, "is a creature very different from the former."

Upon which the Sirian, placing the supposed animal in the hollow of his hand, the passengers and crew, who believed themselves thrown by a hurricane upon some rock, began to put themselves in motion. The sailors having hoisted out some casks of wine, jumped after them into the hand of Micromegas; the mathematicians having secured their quadrants, sectors, and Lapland servants, went overboard at a different place, and made such a bustle in their descent that the Sirian at length felt his fingers tickled by something that seemed to move. An iron bar chanced to penetrate about a foot deep into his forefinger; and from this prick he concluded that something had issued from the little animal he held in his hand; but at first he suspected nothing more, for the microscope, that scarce rendered a whale and a ship visible, had no effect upon an object so imperceptible as man.

I do not intend to shock the vanity of any person whatever; but here I am obliged to request people of importance to consider that, supposing the stature of a man to be about five feet, we mortals make just such a figure upon the earth as an animal the sixty thousandth part of a foot in height would exhibit upon a bowl ten feet in circumference. When you reflect upon a being who could hold this whole earth in the palm of his hand, and is provided with organs proportioned to those we possess, you will easily conceive that there must be a great variety of created substances—and pray, what must such beings think of those battles by which a conqueror gains a small village, to lose it again in the sequel?

I do not at all doubt but if some captain of grenadiers should chance to read this work, he would add two large feet at least to the caps of his company; but I assure him his labor will be in vain, for, do what he will, he and his soldiers will never be other than infinitely diminutive and inconsiderable.

What wonderful address must have been inherent in our Sirian philosopher that enabled him to perceive these atoms of which we have been speaking. When Leuwenhoek and Hartsoeker observed the first rudiments of which we are formed, they did not make such an astonishing discovery. What pleasure, therefore, was the portion of Micromegas in observing the motion of those little machines, in examining all their pranks, and following them in all their operations! With what joy did he put his microscope into his companion's hand; and with what transport did they both at once exclaim:

"I see them distinctly—don't you see them carrying burdens, lying down and rising up again?"

So saying, their hands shook with eagerness to see and apprehension to lose such uncommon objects. The Saturnian, passing from an excess of incredulity to an excess of credulity, thought he saw them mating. "Ah" he said. "I have caught nature in the act." But he was fooled by appearances, which happens only too often, whether one is using a microscope or not.

WHAT HAPPENED IN THEIR INTERCOURSE WITH MEN

Micromegas being a much better observer than the dwarf, perceived distinctly that those atoms spoke; and made the remark to his companion, who was so much ashamed of being mistaken in his first suggestion that he would not believe such a puny species could possibly communicate their ideas, for, though he had the gift of tongues, as well as his companion, he could not hear those particles speak, and, therefore, supposed they had no language.

"Besides, how should such imperceptible beings have the organs of speech? And what in the name of Jove can they say to one another? In order to speak, they must have something like thought, and if they think, they must surely have something equivalent to a soul. Now, to attribute anything like a soul to such an insect species appears a mere absurdity."

"But just now," replied the Sirian, "you believed they were engaged in devotional exercises; and do you think this could be done without thinking, without using some sort of language, or at least some way of making themselves understood? Or do you suppose it is more difficult to advance an argument than to engage in physical exercise? For my own part, I look upon all faculties as alike mysterious."

"I will no longer venture to believe or deny," answered the dwarf, "in short, I have no opinion at all. Let us endeavor to examine these insects, and we will reason upon them afterward."

"With all my heart," said Micromegas, who, taking out a pair of scissors which he kept for paring his nails, cut off a paring from his thumb nail, of which he immediately formed a large kind of speaking trumpet, like a vast tunnel, and clapped the pipe to his ear; as the circumference of this machine included the ship and all the crew, the most feeble voice was conveyed along the circular fibers of the nail; so that, thanks to his industry, the philosopher could distinctly hear the buzzing of our insects that were below. In a few hours he distinguished articulate sounds, and at last plainly understood the French language. The dwarf heard the same, though with more difficulty.

The astonishment of our travelers increased every instant. They heard a nest of mites talk in a very sensible strain: and that lusus naturæ seemed to them inexplicable. You need not doubt but the Sirian and his dwarf glowed with impatience to enter into conversation with such atoms. Micromegas being afraid that his voice, like thunder, would deafen and confound the mites, without being understood by them, saw the necessity of diminishing the sound; each, therefore, put into his mouth a sort of small toothpick, the slender end of which reached to the vessel.

The Sirian setting the dwarf upon his knees, and the ship and crew upon his nail, held down his head and spoke softly. In time, having taken these and a great many more precautions, he addressed himself to them in these words, "O ye invisible insects, whom the hand of the Creator hath deigned to produce in the abyss of infinite littleness! I give praise to His goodness, in that He hath been pleased to disclose unto me those secrets that seemed to be impenetrable."

If ever there was such a thing as astonishment, it seized upon the people who heard this address, and who could not conceive from whence it proceeded. The chaplain of the ship repeated exorcisms, the sailors swore, and the philosophers formed a system; but, notwithstanding all their systems, they could not divine who the person was that spoke to them. Then the dwarf of Saturn, whose voice was softer than that of Micromegas, gave them briefly to understand what species of beings they had to do with. He related the particulars of their voyage from Saturn, made them acquainted with the rank and quality of Monsieur Micromegas, and, after having pitied their smallness, asked if they had always been in that miserable state so near akin to annihilation; and what their business was upon that globe which seemed to be the property of whales. He also desired to know if they were happy in their situation? If they were inspired with souls? And put a hundred questions of the like nature.

A certain mathematician on board, braver than the rest, and shocked to hear his soul called in question, planted his quadrant, and having taken two observations of this interlocutor, said: "You believe then, Mr. what's your name, that because you measure from head to foot a thousand fathoms—"

"A thousand fathoms!" cried the dwarf, "good heavens! How should he know the height of my stature? A thousand fathoms! My very dimensions to a hair. What, measured by a mite! This atom, forsooth, is a geometrician, and knows exactly how tall I am; while I, who can scarce perceive him through a microscope, am utterly ignorant of his extent!"

"Yes, I have taken your measure," answered the philosopher, "and I will now do the same by your tall companion."

The proposal was embraced; his excellency reclined upon his side, for, had he stood upright, his head would have reached too far above the clouds. Our mathematicians planted a tall tree near him, and then, by a series of triangles joined together, they discovered that the object of their observation was a strapping youth, exactly one hundred and twenty thousand royal feet in length. In consequence of this calculation, Micromegas uttered these words:

"I am now more than ever convinced that we ought to judge of nothing by its external magnitude. O God! who hast bestowed understanding upon such seemingly contemptible substances, thou canst with equal ease, produce that which is infinitely small, as that which is incredibly great; and if it be possible that among thy works there are beings still more diminutive than these, they may, nevertheless, be endued with understanding superior to the intelligence of those stupendous animals I have seen in heaven, a single foot of whom is larger than this whole globe on which I have alighted."

One of the philosophers assured him that there were intelligent beings much smaller than men, and recounted not only Virgil's whole fable of the bees, but also described all that Swammerdam had discovered and Reaumur dissected. In a word, he informed him that there are animals which bear the same proportion to bees that bees bear to man, the same as the Sirian himself compared to those vast beings whom he had mentioned, and as those huge animals are to other substances, before whom they would appear like so many particles of dust.

Here the conversation became very interesting, and Micromegas proceeded in these words, "O ye intelligent atoms, in whom the Supreme Being hath been pleased to manifest his omniscience and power, without a doubt your joys on this earth must be pure and exquisite; for, being unincumbered with matter, and, to all appearance, little else than soul, you must spend your lives in the delights of pleasure and reflection, which are the true enjoyments of a perfect spirit. True happiness I have nowhere found; but certainly, here it dwells."

At this harangue all the philosophers shook their heads, and one among them, more candid than his brethren, frankly owned that, excepting a very small number of inhabitants who were very little esteemed by their fellows, all the rest were a parcel of knaves, fools, and miserable wretches.

"We have matter enough," said he, "to do abundance of mischief, if mischief comes from matter; and too much understanding, if evil flows from understanding. You must know, for example, that at this very moment, while I am speaking, there are one hundred thousand animals of our own species, covered with hats, slaying an equal number of their fellow-creatures who wear turbans; at least they are either slaying or being slain; and this hath usually been the case all over the earth from time immemorial."

The Sirian, shuddering at this information, begged to know the cause of those horrible quarrels among such a puny race, and was given to understand that the subject of the dispute was a pitiful mole-hill (called Palestine), no larger than his heel. Not that any one of those millions who cut one another's throats pretends to have the least claim to the smallest particle of that clod. The question is, whether it shall belong to a certain person who is known by the name of Sultan, or to another whom (for what reason I know not) they dignify with the appellation of Pope. Neither the one nor the other has seen or ever will see the pitiful corner in question; and probably none of these wretches, who so madly destroy each other, ever beheld the ruler on whose account they are so mercilessly sacrificed!

"Ah, miscreants!" cried the indignant Sirian, "Such excess

of desperate rage is beyond conception. I have a good mind to take two or three steps, and trample the whole nest of such ridiculous assassins under my feet."

"Don't give yourself the trouble," replied the philosopher; "they are industrious enough in procuring their own destruction. At the end of ten years the hundredth part of those wretches will not survive; for you must know that, though they should not draw a sword in the cause they have espoused, famine, fatigue, and intemperance would sweep almost all of them from the face of the earth. Besides, the punishment should not be inflicted upon them, but upon those sedentary and slothful barbarians, who, from their palaces, give orders for murdering a million of men and then solemnly thank God for their success."

Our traveler was moved with compassion for the entire human race, in which he discovered such astonishing contrasts. "Since you are of the small number of the wise," said he, "and in all likelihood do not engage yourselves in the trade of murder for hire, be so good as to tell me your occupation."

"We anatomize flies," replied the philosopher, "we measure lines, we make calculations, we agree upon two or three points which we understand, and dispute upon two or three thousand that are beyond our comprehension."

"How far," said the Sirian, "do you reckon the distance between the great star of the constellation Gemini and that called Canicula?"

To this question all of them answered with one voice: "Thirty-two degrees and a half."

"And what is the distance from thence to the moon?"

"Sixty semi-diameters of the earth."

He then thought to puzzle them by asking the weight of the air; but they answered distinctly that common air is about nine hundred times specifically lighter than an equal column of the lightest water, and nineteen hundred times lighter than current gold. The little dwarf of Saturn, astonished at their answers, was now tempted to believe those people sorcerers who, but a quarter of an hour before, he would not allow were inspired with souls.

"Well," said Micromegas, "since you know so well what is without you, doubtless you are still more perfectly acquainted with that which is within. Tell me what is the soul, and how do your ideas originate?"

Here the philosophers spoke altogether as before; but each was of a different opinion. The eldest quoted Aristotle, another pronounced the name of Descartes, a third mentioned Malebranche, a fourth Leibnitz, and a fifth Locke. An old peripatetic, lifting up his voice, exclaimed with an air of confidence: "The soul is perfection and reason, having power to be such as it is, as Aristotle expressly declares, page 633, of the Louvre edition:

"Εντελεῖά τις ἐστί, χαὶ λόγος τοῦ δύναμτιν ἔχοντος τοιοῦδι εἶταῖ"

"I am not very well versed in Greek," said the giant.

"Nor I, either," replied the philosophical mite.

"Why, then, do you quote that same Aristotle in Greek," resumed the Sirian.

"Because," answered the other, "it is but reasonable we should quote what we do not comprehend in a language we do not understand."

Here the Cartesian interposing: "The soul," said he, "is a pure spirit or intelligence, which hath received before birth all the metaphysical ideas; but after that event it is obliged to go to school and learn anew the knowledge which it hath lost."

"So it is necessary," replied the animal of eight leagues, "that thy soul should be learned before birth, in order to be so ignorant when thou hast got a beard upon thy chin. But what dost thou understand by spirit?"

"I have no idea of it," said the philosopher; "indeed, it is supposed to be immaterial."

"At least, thou knowest what matter is?" resumed the Sirian.

"Perfectly well," answered the other, "for example: that stone is gray, is of a certain figure, has three dimensions, specific weight, and divisibility."

"I want to know," said the giant, "what that object is, which, according to thy observation, hath a gray color, weight and divisibility. Thou seest a few qualities, but dost thou know the nature of the thing itself?"

"Not I, truly," answered the Cartesian.

Upon which the Sirian admitted that he also was ignorant in regard to this subject. Then addressing himself to another sage, who stood upon his thumb, he asked: "What is the soul? And what are its functions?"

"Nothing at all," replied this disciple of Malebranche; "God hath made everything for my convenience. In Him I see everything, by Him I act; He is the universal agent, and I never meddle in His work."

"That is being a nonentity indeed," said the Sirian sage; and then, turning to a follower of Leibnitz, he exclaimed: "Hark ye, friend, what is thy opinion of the soul?"

"In my opinion," answered this metaphysician, "the soul is the hand that points at the hour, while my body does the office of the clock; or, if you please, the soul is the clock, and the body is the pointer; or again, my soul is the mirror of the universe, and my body the frame. All this is clear and incontrovertible."

A little partisan of Locke, who chanced to be present, being asked his opinion on the same subject, said, "I do not know by what power I think; but well I know that I should never have thought without the assistance of my senses. That there are immaterial and intelligent substances I do not at all doubt; but that it is impossible for God to communicate the faculty of thinking to matter, I doubt very much. I revere the Eternal Power, to which it would ill become me to prescribe bounds. I affirm nothing, and am contented to believe that many more things are possible than are usually thought so."

The Sirian smiled at this declaration, and did not look upon the author as the least sagacious of the company; and as for the dwarf of Saturn, he would have embraced this adherent of Locke, had it not been for the extreme disproportion in their respective sizes. But unluckily there was another animalcule in a square cap, who, taking the word from all his philosophical brethren, affirmed that he knew the whole secret, which was contained in the abridgment of St. Thomas. He surveyed the two celestial strangers from top to toe, and maintained to their faces that their persons, their fashions, their suns, and their stars were created solely for the use of man.

At this wild assertion our two travelers were seized with a fit of that uncontrollable laughter, which (according to Homer) is the portion of the immortal gods; their bellies quivered, their shoulders rose and fell, and, during these convulsions, the vessel fell from the Sirian's nail into the Saturnian's pocket, where these worthy people searched for it a long time with great diligence. At length, having found the ship and set everything to rights again, the Sirian resumed the discourse with those diminutive mites, and promised to compose for them a choice book of philosophy which would demonstrate the very essence of things.

Accordingly, before his departure, he made them a present of the book, which was brought to the Academy of Sciences at Paris, but when the old secretary came to open it, he saw nothing but blank paper, upon which—

"Ay, ay," said he, "this is just what I suspected."

Plato's Dream

PLATO'S DREAM

In ancient times, dreams were much revered, and Plato was one of the greatest dreamers. His dream The Republic is deservedly famous, but the following little-known tale is perhaps his most amazing dream—or nightmare:

The great Demiurgos, the eternal geometer, having scattered throughout the immensity of space innumerable worlds, decided to test the knowledge of those lesser superbeings who were also his creations, and who had witnessed his works. He gave them each a small portion of matter to arrange, just as our own art teachers give their students a statue to carve, or a picture to paint, if we may compare small things to great.

Demogorgon received the lump of mold we call Earth, and having formed it as it now appears, thought he had created a masterpiece. He imagined he had silenced Envy herself, and expected to receive the highest praise, even from his brethren. How great was his surprise, when, at the presentation of his work, they hissed in disapproval!

One among them, more sarcastic than the rest, spoke:

"Truly you have performed mighty feats! You have divided

your world into two parts; and, to prevent them from communicating with each other, placed a vast collection of waters between the two hemispheres. The inhabitants must perish with cold under both your poles, and be scorched to death under the equator. You have, in your great prudence, formed immense deserts of sand, so all who travel over them may die with hunger and thirst. I have no fault to find with your cows, sheep, cocks, and hens; but can never be reconciled to your serpents and spiders. Your onions and artichokes are very good things, but I cannot conceive what induced you to scatter such a heap of poisonous plants over the face of the planet, unless it was to poison its inhabitants. Moreover, if I am not mistaken, you have created about 30 different kinds of monkeys, a still greater number of dogs, yet only four or five races of humans. It is true, indeed, you have bestowed on the latter of these animals a faculty you call Reason, but it is so poorly executed that you might better call it Folly. Besides, you do not seem to have shown any very great regard for this two-legged creature, seeing you have left him with so few means of defense; subjected him to so many disorders, and provided him with so few remedies; and formed him with such a multitude of passions, and so little wisdom and prudence to resist them. You certainly were not willing that there should remain any great number of these animals on Earth at once; for, over the course of a given year, smallpox will regularly carry off a tenth of the species, and sister maladies will taint the springs of life in the remainder; and then, as if this was not enough, you have so disposed things that half of those who survive are occupied in lawsuits, or cutting each others' throats. Yes, they must be infinitely grateful to you, and I must admit that you have executed a masterpiece."

Demogorgon blushed. He now realized there was much moral and physical evil in his work, but still believed it contained more good than ill.

"It is easy to find fault," he said; "but do you imagine it is so easy to form an animal, who, having the gift of reason and free will, shall not sometimes abuse his liberty? Do you think that, in rearing 10,000 plants, it is so easy to prevent some few from having noxious qualities? Do you suppose that, with a certain quantity of water, sand, and mud, you could make a globe without sea or desert?

"As for you, my sneering friend, I think you have just finished the planet Jupiter. Let us see now what figure you make with your great belts, and your long nights, with four moons to enlighten them. Let us examine your worlds, and see whether the inhabitants you have made are exempt from folly and disease."

Accordingly, his fellow entities examined the planet Jupiter, and were soon laughing at the laugher. He who had made Saturn did not escape without his share of censure, and his fellows, the makers of Mars, Mercury, and Venus, was each in his turn reproached.

They were in the midst of railing against and ridiculing each other, when the eternal Demiurgos thus imposed silence on them all:

"In your performances there is both good and bad, because you have a great share of understanding, but at the same time fall short of perfection. Your works will endure for only a few billion years, after which you will acquire more knowledge and perform much better. It belongs to me alone to create things perfect and immortal."

"Us, for example?" asked Demogorgon.

Demiurgos scowled, and with that Plato awoke.

Or did he?

Candide

HOW CANDIDE WAS BROUGHT UP IN A MAGNIFICENT CASTLE, AND HOW HE WAS EXPELLED THENCE

In a castle of Westphalia, belonging to the Baron of Thunder-ten-Tronckh, lived a youth, whom nature had endowed with the most gentle manners. His countenance was a true picture of his soul. He combined a true judgment with simplicity of spirit, which was the reason, I apprehend, of his being called Candide. The old servants of the family suspected him to have been the son of the Baron's sister, by a good, honest gentleman of the neighborhood, whom that young lady would never marry because he had been able to prove only seventy-one quarterings, the rest of his genealogical tree having been lost through the injuries of time.

The Baron was one of the most powerful lords in Westphalia, for his castle had not only a gate, but windows. His great hall, even, was hung with tapestry. All the dogs of his farmyards formed a pack of hounds at need; his grooms were his huntsmen; and the curate of the village was his grand almoner. They called him "My Lord," and laughed at all his stories.

The Baron's lady weighed about three hundred and fifty pounds, and was therefore a person of great consideration, and she did the honours of the house with a dignity that commanded still greater respect. Her daughter Cunegonde was seventeen years of age, fresh-coloured, comely, plump, and desirable. The Baron's son seemed to be in every respect worthy of his father. The Preceptor Pangloss was the oracle of the family, and little Candide heard his lessons with all the good faith of his age and character.

Pangloss was professor of metaphysico-theologico-cosmolo-ingology. He proved admirably that there is no effect without a cause, and that, in this best of all possible worlds, the Baron's castle was the most magnificent of castles, and his lady the best of all possible Baronesses.

"It is demonstrable," said he, "that things cannot be otherwise than as they are; for all being created for an end, all is necessarily for the best end. Observe, that the nose has been formed to bear spectacles—thus we have spectacles. Legs are visibly designed for stockings—and we have stockings. Stones were made to be hewn, and to construct castles—therefore my lord has a magnificent castle; for the greatest baron in the province ought to be the best lodged. Pigs were made to be eaten—therefore we eat pork all the year round. Consequently, they who assert that all is well have said a foolish thing, they should have said all is for the best."

Candide listened attentively and believed innocently; for he thought Miss Cunegonde extremely beautiful, though he never had the courage to tell her so. He concluded that after the happiness of being born of Baron of Thunder-ten-Tronckh, the second degree of happiness was to be Miss Cunegonde, the third that of seeing her every day, and the fourth that of hearing Master Pangloss, the greatest philosopher of the whole province, and consequently of the whole world.

One day Cunegonde, while walking near the castle, in a little wood which they called a park, saw between the bushes,

Dr. Pangloss giving a lesson in experimental natural philosophy to her mother's chamber-maid, a little brown wench, very pretty and very docile. As Miss Cunegonde had a great disposition for the sciences, she breathlessly observed the repeated experiments of which she was a witness; she clearly perceived the force of the Doctor's reasons, the effects, and the causes; she turned back greatly flurried, quite pensive, and filled with the desire to be learned; dreaming that she might well be a sufficient reason for young Candide, and he for her.

She met Candide on reaching the castle and blushed; Candide blushed also; she wished him good morrow in a faltering tone, and Candide spoke to her without knowing what he said. The next day after dinner, as they went from table, Cunegonde and Candide found themselves behind a screen; Cunegonde let fall her handkerchief, Candide picked it up, she took him innocently by the hand, the youth as innocently kissed the young lady's hand with particular vivacity, sensibility, and grace; their lips met, their eyes sparkled, their knees trembled, their hands strayed. Baron Thunder-ten-Tronckh passed near the screen and beholding this cause and effect chased Candide from the castle with great kicks on the backside; Cunegonde fainted away; she was boxed on the ears by the Baroness, as soon as she came to herself; and all was consternation in this most magnificent and most agreeable of all possible castles.

WHAT BECAME OF CANDIDE AMONG THE BULGARIANS

Candide, driven from terrestrial paradise, walked a long while without knowing where, weeping, raising his eyes to heaven, turning them often towards the most magnificent of castles which imprisoned the purest of noble young ladies. He lay down to sleep without supper, in the middle of a field between two furrows. The snow fell in large flakes. The next day Candide, all benumbed, dragged himself towards the neighbouring town which was called Waldberghofftrarbk-dikdorff, having no money, dying of hunger and fatigue, he stopped sorrowfully at the door of an inn. Two men dressed in blue observed him. "Comrade," said one, "here is a well-built young fellow, and of proper height."

They went up to Candide and very civilly invited him to dinner.

"Gentlemen," replied Candide, with a most engaging modesty, "you do me great honour, but I have not wherewithal to pay my share."

"Oh, sir," said one of the blues to him, "people of your

appearance and of your merit never pay anything: are you not five feet five inches high?"

"Yes, sir, that is my height," answered he, making a low bow.

"Come, sir, seat yourself; not only will we pay your reckoning, but we will never suffer such a man as you to want money; men are only born to assist one another."

"You are right," said Candide; "this is what I was always taught by Mr. Pangloss, and I see plainly that all is for the best."

They begged of him to accept a few crowns. He took them, and wished to give them his note; they refused; they seated themselves at table.

"Love you not deeply?"

"Oh yes," answered he; "I deeply love Miss Cunegonde."

"No," said one of the gentlemen, "we ask you if you do not deeply love the King of the Bulgarians?"

"Not at all," said he; "for I have never seen him."

"What! he is the best of kings, and we must drink his health."

"Oh! very willingly, gentlemen," and he drank.

"That is enough," they tell him. "Now you are the help, the support, the defender, the hero of the Bulgarians. Your fortune is made, and your glory is assured."

Instantly they fettered him, and carried him away to the regiment. There he was made to wheel about to the right, and to the left, to draw his rammer, to return his rammer, to present, to fire, to march, and they gave him thirty blows with a cudgel. The next day he did his exercise a little less badly, and he received but twenty blows. The day following they gave him only ten, and he was regarded by his comrades as a prodigy.

Candide, all stupefied, could not yet very well realise how he was a hero. He resolved one fine day in spring to go for a walk, marching straight before him, believing that it was a privilege of the human as well as of the animal species to make use of their legs as they pleased. He had advanced two leagues when he was overtaken by four others, heroes of six feet, who bound him and carried him to a dungeon. He was asked which he would like the best, to be whipped six-and-thirty times through all the regiment, or to receive at once twelve balls of lead in his brain. He vainly said that human will is free, and that he chose neither the one nor the other. He was forced to make a choice; he determined, in virtue of that gift of God called liberty, to run the gauntlet six-and-thirty times. He bore this twice. The regiment was composed of two thousand men; that composed for him four thousand strokes, which laid bare all his muscles and nerves, from the nape of his neck quite down to his rump. As they were going to proceed to a third whipping, Candide, able to bear no more, begged as a favour that they would be so good as to shoot him. He obtained this favour; they bandaged his eyes, and bade him kneel down. The King of the Bulgarians passed at this moment and ascertained the nature of the crime. As he had great talent, he understood from all that he learnt of Candide that he was a young meta-physician, extremely ignorant of the things of this world, and he accorded him his pardon with a clemency which will bring him praise in all the journals, and throughout all ages.

An able surgeon cured Candide in three weeks by means of emollients taught by Dioscorides. He had already a little skin, and was able to march when the King of the Bulgarians gave battle to the King of the Abares.

HOW CANDIDE MADE
HIS ESCAPE FROM THE
BULGARIANS, AND WHAT
AFTERWARDS BECAME OF HIM

There was never anything so gallant, so spruce, so brilliant, and so well disposed as the two armies. Trumpets, fifes, hautboys, drums, and cannon made music such as Hell itself had never heard. The cannons first of all laid flat about six thousand men on each side; the muskets swept away from this best of worlds nine or ten thousand ruffians who infested its surface. The bayonet was also a sufficient reason for the death of several thousands. The whole might amount to thirty thousand souls. Candide, who trembled like a philosopher, hid himself as well as he could during this heroic butchery.

At length, while the two kings were causing Te Deum to be sung each in his own camp, Candide resolved to go and reason elsewhere on effects and causes. He passed over heaps of dead and dying, and first reached a neighbouring village; it was in cinders, it was an Abare village which the Bulgarians had burnt according to the laws of war. Here, old men covered with wounds, beheld their wives, hugging their children to their bloody breasts, massacred before their faces; there, their daughters, disemboweled and breathing their last after having satisfied the natural wants of Bulgarian heroes; while others, half burnt in the flames, begged to be despatched. The earth was strewed with brains, arms, and legs.

Candide fled quickly to another village; it belonged to the Bulgarians; and the Abarian heroes had treated it in the same way. Candide, walking always over palpitating limbs or across ruins, arrived at last beyond the seat of war, with a few provisions in his knapsack, and Miss Cunegonde always in his heart. His provisions failed him when he arrived in Holland; but having heard that everybody was rich in that country, and that they were Christians, he did not doubt but he should meet with the same treatment from them as he had met with in the Baron's castle, before Miss Cunegonde's bright eyes were the cause of his expulsion thence.

He asked alms of several grave-looking people, who all answered him, that if he continued to follow this trade they would confine him to the house of correction, where he should be taught to get a living.

The next he addressed was a man who had been haranguing a large assembly for a whole hour on the subject of charity. But the orator, looking askew, said:

"What are you doing here? Are you for the good cause?"

"There can be no effect without a cause," modestly answered Candide; "the whole is necessarily concatenated and arranged for the best. It was necessary for me to have been banished from the presence of Miss Cunegonde, to have afterwards run the gauntlet, and now it is necessary I should beg my bread until I learn to earn it; all this cannot be otherwise."

"My friend," said the orator to him, "do you believe the Pope to be Anti-Christ?"

"I have not heard it," answered Candide; "but whether he be, or whether he be not, I want bread."

"Thou dost not deserve to eat," said the other. "Begone, rogue; begone, wretch; do not come near me again."

The orator's wife, putting her head out of the window, and spying a man that doubted whether the Pope was Anti-Christ, poured over him a full..."Oh, heavens! to what excess does religious zeal carry the ladies."

A man who had never been christened, a good Anabaptist, named James, beheld the cruel and ignominious treatment shown to one of his brethren, an unfeathered biped with a rational soul, he took him home, cleaned him, gave him bread and beer, presented him with two florins, and even wished to teach him the manufacture of Persian stuffs which they make in Holland. Candide, almost prostrating himself before him, cried:

"Master Pangloss has well said that all is for the best in this world, for I am infinitely more touched by your extreme generosity than with the inhumanity of that gentleman in the black coat and his lady."

The next day, as he took a walk, he met a beggar all covered with scabs, his eyes diseased, the end of his nose eaten away, his mouth distorted, his teeth black, choking in his throat, tormented with a violent cough, and spitting out a tooth at each effort.

HOW CANDIDE FOUND HIS OLD MASTER PANGLOSS, AND WHAT HAPPENED TO THEM

Candide, yet more moved with compassion than with horror, gave to this shocking beggar the two florins which he had received from the honest Anabaptist James. The spectre looked at him very earnestly, dropped a few tears, and fell upon his neck. Candide recoiled in disgust.

"Alas!" said one wretch to the other, "Do you no longer know your dear Pangloss?"

"What do I hear? You, my dear master! You in this terrible plight! What misfortune has happened to you? Why are you no longer in the most magnificent of castles? What has become of Miss Cunegonde, the pearl of girls, and nature's masterpiece?"

"I am so weak that I cannot stand," said Pangloss.

Upon which Candide carried him to the Anabaptist's stable, and gave him a crust of bread. As soon as Pangloss had refreshed himself a little:

"Well," said Candide, "Cunegonde?"

"She is dead," replied the other.

Candide fainted at this word; his friend recalled his senses with a little bad vinegar which he found by chance in the stable. Candide reopened his eyes.

"Cunegonde is dead! Ah, best of worlds, where art thou? But of what illness did she die? Was it not for grief, upon seeing her father kick me out of his magnificent castle?"

"No," said Pangloss, "she was ripped open by the Bulgarian soldiers, after having been violated by many; they broke the Baron's head for attempting to defend her; my lady, her mother, was cut in pieces; my poor pupil was served just in the same manner as his sister; and as for the castle, they have not left one stone upon another, not a barn, nor a sheep, nor a duck, nor a tree; but we have had our revenge, for the Abares have done the very same thing to a neighbouring barony, which belonged to a Bulgarian lord."

At this discourse Candide fainted again; but coming to himself, and having said all that it became him to say, inquired into the cause and effect, as well as into the sufficient reason that had reduced Pangloss to so miserable a plight.

"Alas!" said the other, "it was love; love, the comfort of the human species, the preserver of the universe, the soul of all sensible beings, love, tender love."

"Alas!" said Candide, "I know this love, that sovereign of hearts, that soul of our souls; yet it never cost me more than a kiss and twenty kicks on the backside. How could this beautiful cause produce in you an effect so abominable?"

Pangloss made answer in these terms: "Oh, my dear Candide, you remember Paquette, that pretty wench who waited on our noble Baroness; in her arms I tasted the delights of paradise, which produced in me those hell torments with which you see me devoured; she was infected with them, she is perhaps dead of them. This present Paquette received of a learned Grey Friar, who had traced it to its source; he had had it of an old countess, who had received it from a cavalry captain, who owed it to a marchioness, who took it from a page, who had received it from a Jesuit, who when a novice had it in a direct line from one of the companions of Christopher Columbus. For my part I shall give it to nobody, I am dying."

"Oh, Pangloss!" cried Candide, "what a strange genealogy! Is not the Devil the original stock of it?"

"Not at all," replied this great man, "it was a thing unavoidable, a necessary ingredient in the best of worlds; for if Columbus had not in an island of America caught this disease, which contaminates the source of life, frequently even hinders generation, and which is evidently opposed to the great end of nature, we should have neither chocolate nor cochineal. We are also to observe that upon our continent, this distemper is like religious controversy, confined to a particular spot. The Turks, the Indians, the Persians, the Chinese, the Siamese, the Japanese, know nothing of it; but there is a sufficient reason for believing that they will know it in their turn in a few centuries. In the meantime, it has made marvellous progress among us, especially in those great armies composed of honest well-disciplined hirelings, who decide the destiny of states; for we may safely affirm that when an army of thirty thousand men fights another of an equal number, there are about twenty thousand of them poxed on each side."

"Well, this is wonderful!" said Candide, "but you must get cured."

"Alas! how can I?" said Pangloss, "I have not a farthing, my friend, and all over the globe there is no letting of blood or taking a glister, without paying, or somebody paying for you."

These last words determined Candide; he went and flung himself at the feet of the charitable Anabaptist James, and gave him so touching a picture of the state to which his friend was reduced, that the good man did not scruple to take Dr. Pangloss into his house, and had him cured at his expense. In the cure

Pangloss lost only an eye and an ear. He wrote well, and knew arithmetic perfectly. The Anabaptist James made him his bookkeeper. At the end of two months, being obliged to go to Lisbon about some mercantile affairs, he took the two philosophers with him in his ship. Pangloss explained to him how everything was so constituted that it could not be better. James was not of this opinion.

"It is more likely," said he, "that humans have a little corrupted nature, for they were not born wolves, and they have become wolves; God has given them neither cannon of four-and-twenty pounders, nor bayonets; and yet they have made cannon and bayonets to destroy one another. Into this account I might throw not only bankrupts, but justice which seizes on the effects of bankrupts to cheat the creditors."

"All this was indispensable," replied the one-eyed doctor, "for private misfortunes make the general good, so that the more private misfortunes there are the greater is the general good."

While he reasoned, the sky darkened, the winds blew from the four quarters, and the ship was assailed by a most terrible tempest within sight of the port of Lisbon.

TEMPEST, SHIPWRECK, EARTHQUAKE, AND WHAT BECAME OF DOCTOR PANGLOSS, CANDIDE, AND JAMES THE ANABAPTIST

Half dead of that inconceivable anguish which the rolling of a ship produces, one-half of the passengers were not even sensible of the danger. The other half shrieked and prayed. The sheets were rent, the masts broken, the vessel gaped. Work who would, no one heard, no one commanded. The Anabaptist being upon deck bore a hand; when a brutish sailor struck him roughly and laid him sprawling; but with the violence of the blow, he himself tumbled head foremost overboard, and stuck upon a piece of the broken mast. Honest James ran to his assistance, hauled him up, and from the effort he made was precipitated into the sea in sight of the sailor, who left him to perish, without deigning to look at him. Candide drew near and saw his benefactor, who rose above the water one moment and was then swallowed up for ever. He was just going to jump after him, but was prevented by the philosopher Pangloss, who demonstrated to him that the Bay of Lisbon had been made on purpose for the Anabaptist to be drowned. While he was proving this à priori, the ship foundered; all perished except Pangloss,

Candide, and that brutal sailor who had drowned the good Anabaptist. The villain swam safely to the shore, while Pangloss and Candide were borne thither upon a plank.

As soon as they recovered themselves a little they walked toward Lisbon. They had some money left, with which they hoped to save themselves from starving, after they had escaped drowning. Scarcely had they reached the city, lamenting the death of their benefactor, when they felt the earth tremble under their feet. The sea swelled and foamed in the harbour, and beat to pieces the vessels riding at anchor. Whirlwinds of fire and ashes covered the streets and public places; houses fell, roofs were flung upon the pavements, and the pavements were scattered. Thirty thousand inhabitants of all ages and sexes were crushed under the ruins. The sailor, whistling and swearing, said there was booty to be gained here.

"What can be the sufficient reason of this phenomenon?" said Pangloss.

"This is the Last Day!" cried Candide.

The sailor ran among the ruins, facing death to find money; finding it, he took it, got drunk, and having slept himself sober, purchased the favours of the first good-natured wench whom he met on the ruins of the destroyed houses, and in the midst of the dying and the dead. Pangloss pulled him by the sleeve.

"My friend," said he, "this is not right. You sin against the universal reason; you choose your time badly."

"S'blood and fury!" answered the other; "I am a sailor and born at Batavia. Four times have I trampled upon the crucifix in four voyages to Japan; a fig for thy universal reason."

Some falling stones had wounded Candide. He lay stretched in the street covered with rubbish.

"Alas!" said he to Pangloss, "get me a little wine and oil; I am dying."

"This concussion of the earth is no new thing," answered

Pangloss. "The city of Lima, in America, experienced the same convulsions last year; the same cause, the same effects; there is certainly a train of sulphur under ground from Lima to Lisbon."

"Nothing more probable," said Candide; "but for the love of God a little oil and wine."

"How, probable?" replied the philosopher. "I maintain that the point is capable of being demonstrated."

Candide fainted away, and Pangloss fetched him some water from a neighbouring fountain. The following day they rummaged among the ruins and found provisions, with which they repaired their exhausted strength. After this they joined with others in relieving those inhabitants who had escaped death. Some, whom they had succoured, gave them as good a dinner as they could in such disastrous circumstances; true, the repast was mournful, and the company moistened their bread with tears; but Pangloss consoled them, assuring them that things could not be otherwise.

"For," said he, "all that is is for the best. If there is a volcano at Lisbon it cannot be elsewhere. It is impossible that things should be other than they are; for everything is right."

A little man dressed in black, Familiar of the Inquisition, who sat by him, politely took up his word and said:

"Apparently, then, sir, you do not believe in original sin; for if all is for the best there has then been neither Fall nor punishment."

"I humbly ask your Excellency's pardon," answered Pangloss, still more politely; "for the Fall and curse of man necessarily entered into the system of the best of worlds."

"Sir," said the Familiar, "you do not then believe in liberty?"

"Your Excellency will excuse me," said Pangloss; "liberty is consistent with absolute necessity, for it was necessary we should be free; for, in short, the determinate will—"

Pangloss was in the middle of his sentence, when the Familiar beckoned to his footman, who gave him a glass of wine from Porto or Opporto.

HOW THE PORTUGUESE MADE A BEAUTIFUL AUTO-DA-FÉ, TO PREVENT ANY FURTHER EARTHQUAKES; AND HOW CANDIDE WAS PUBLICLY WHIPPED

After the earthquake had destroyed three-fourths of Lisbon, the sages of that country could think of no means more effectual to prevent utter ruin than to give the people a beautiful auto-da-fé; for it had been decided by the University of Coimbra, that the burning of a few people alive by a slow fire, and with great ceremony, is an infallible secret to hinder the earth from quaking.

In consequence hereof, they had seized on a Biscayner, convicted of having married his godmother, and on two Portuguese, for rejecting the bacon which larded a chicken they were eating; after dinner, they came and secured Dr. Pangloss, and his disciple Candide, the one for speaking his mind, the other for having listened with an air of approbation. They were conducted to separate apartments, extremely cold, as they were never incommoded by the sun. Eight days after they were dressed in san-benitos and their heads ornamented with paper mitres. The mitre and san-benito belonging to Candide were painted with reversed flames and with devils that had neither tails nor claws; but Pangloss's devils had claws and tails and the flames were upright. They marched in procession thus habited and heard a very pathetic sermon, followed by fine church music. Candide was whipped in cadence while they were singing; the Biscayner, and the two men who had refused to eat bacon, were burnt; and Pangloss was hanged, though that was not the custom. The same day the earth sustained a most violent concussion.

Candide, terrified, amazed, desperate, all bloody, all palpitating, said to himself:

"If this is the best of possible worlds, what then are the others? Well, if I had been only whipped I could put up with it, for I experienced that among the Bulgarians; but oh, my dear Pangloss! thou greatest of philosophers, that I should have seen you hanged, without knowing for what! Oh, my dear Anabaptist, thou best of men, that thou should'st have been drowned in the very harbour! Oh, Miss Cunegonde, thou pearl of girls! that thou should'st have had thy belly ripped open!"

Thus he was musing, scarce able to stand, preached at, whipped, absolved, and blessed, when an old woman accosted him saying:

"My son, take courage and follow me."

HOW THE OLD WOMAN TOOK CARE OF CANDIDE, AND HOW HE FOUND THE OBJECT HE LOVED

Candide did not take courage, but followed the old woman to a decayed house, where she gave him a pot of pomatum to anoint his sores, showed him a very neat little bed, with a suit of clothes hanging up, and left him something to eat and drink.

"Eat, drink, sleep," said she, "and may our lady of Atocha, the great St. Anthony of Padua, and the great St. James of Compostella, receive you under their protection. I shall be back to-morrow."

Candide, amazed at all he had suffered and still more with the charity of the old woman, wished to kiss her hand.

"It is not my hand you must kiss," said the old woman; "I shall be back to-morrow. Anoint yourself with the pomatum, eat and sleep."

Candide, notwithstanding so many disasters, ate and slept. The next morning the old woman brought him his breakfast, looked at his back, and rubbed it herself with another ointment: in like manner she brought him his dinner; and at night she returned with his supper. The day following she went through the very same ceremonies.

"Who are you?" said Candide; "who has inspired you with so much goodness? What return can I make you?"

The good woman made no answer; she returned in the evening, but brought no supper.

"Come with me," she said, "and say nothing."

She took him by the arm, and walked with him about a quarter of a mile into the country; they arrived at a lonely house, surrounded with gardens and canals. The old woman knocked at a little door, it opened, she led Candide up a private staircase into a small apartment richly furnished. She left him on a brocaded sofa, shut the door and went away. Candide thought himself in a dream; indeed, that he had been dreaming unluckily all his life, and that the present moment was the only agreeable part of it all.

The old woman returned very soon, supporting with difficulty a trembling woman of a majestic figure, brilliant with jewels, and covered with a veil.

"Take off that veil," said the old woman to Candide.

The young man approached, he rose the veil with a timid hand. Oh! what a moment! what surprise! He believed he beheld Miss Cunegonde? He really saw her! It is herself! His strength failed him, he cannot utter a word, but dropped at her feet. Cunegonde fell upon the sofa. The old woman supplied a smelling bottle; they came to themselves and recovered their speech. As they began with broken accents, with questions and answers interchangeably interrupted with sighs, with tears, and cries, the old woman desired they would make less noise and then she left them to themselves.

"What, is it you?" said Candide, "You live? I find you again in Portugal? Then you have not been ravished? Then they did not rip open your belly as Doctor Pangloss informed me?"

"Yes, they did," said the beautiful Cunegonde; "but those two accidents are not always mortal."

"But were your father and mother killed?"

"It is but too true," answered Cunegonde, in tears.

"And your brother?"

"My brother also was killed."

"And why are you in Portugal? And how did you know of my being here? And by what strange adventure did you contrive to bring me to this house?"

"I will tell you all that," replied the lady, "but first of all let me know your history, since the innocent kiss you gave me and the kicks which you received."

Candide respectfully obeyed her, and though he was still in a surprise, though his voice was feeble and trembling, though his back still pained him, yet he gave her a most ingenuous account of everything that had befallen him since the moment of their separation. Cunegonde lifted up her eyes to heaven; shed tears upon hearing of the death of the good Anabaptist and of Pangloss; after which she spoke as follows to Candide, who did not lose a word and devoured her with his eyes.

THE HISTORY OF CUNEGONDE

"I was in bed and fast asleep when it pleased God to send the Bulgarians to our delightful castle of Thunder-ten-Tronckh; they slew my father and brother, and cut my mother in pieces. A tall Bulgarian, six feet high, perceiving that I had fainted away at this sight, began to ravish me; this made me recover; I regained my senses, I cried, I struggled, I bit, I scratched, I wanted to tear out the tall Bulgarian's eyes—not knowing that what happened at my father's house was the usual practice of war. The brute gave me a cut in the left side with his hanger, and the mark is still upon me."

"Ah! I hope I shall see it," said honest Candide.

"You shall," said Cunegonde, "but let us continue."

"Do so," replied Candide.

Thus she resumed the thread of her story:

"A Bulgarian captain came in, saw me all bleeding, and the soldier not in the least disconcerted. The captain flew into a passion at the disrespectful behaviour of the brute, and slew him on my body. He ordered my wounds to be dressed, and took me to his quarters as a prisoner of war. I washed the few shirts that he had, I did his cooking; he thought me very pretty —he avowed it; on the other hand, I must own he had a good shape, and a soft and white skin; but he had little or no mind or philosophy, and you might see plainly that he had never been instructed by Doctor Pangloss. In three months' time, having lost all his money, and being grown tired of my company, he sold me to a Jew, named Don Issachar, who traded to Holland and Portugal, and had a strong passion for women. This Jew was much attached to my person, but could not triumph over it; I resisted him better than the Bulgarian soldier. A modest woman may be ravished once, but her virtue is strengthened by it. In order to render me more tractable, he brought me to this country house. Hitherto I had imagined that nothing could equal the beauty of Thunder-ten-Tronckh Castle; but I found I was mistaken."

"The Grand Inquisitor, seeing me one day at Mass, stared long at me, and sent to tell me that he wished to speak on private matters. I was conducted to his palace, where I acquainted him with the history of my family, and he represented to me how much it was beneath my rank to belong to an Israelite. A proposal was then made to Don Issachar that he should resign me to my lord. Don Issachar, being the court banker, and a man of credit, would hear nothing of it. The Inquisitor threatened him with an auto-da-fé. At last my Jew, intimidated, concluded a bargain, by which the house and myself should belong to both in common; the Jew should have for himself Monday, Wednesday, and Saturday, and the Inquisitor should have the rest of the week. It is now six months since this agreement was made. Quarrels have not been wanting, for they could not decide whether the night from Saturday to Sunday belonged to the old law or to the new. For my part, I have so far held out against both, and I verily believe that this is the reason why I am still beloved."

"At length, to avert the scourge of earthquakes, and to intimidate Don Issachar, my Lord Inquisitor was pleased to celebrate an auto-da-fé. He did me the honour to invite me to the ceremony. I had a very good seat, and the ladies were served with refreshments between Mass and the execution. I was in truth seized with horror at the burning of those two Jews, and of the honest Biscayner who had married his godmother; but what was my surprise, my fright, my trouble, when I saw in a san-benito and mitre a figure which resembled that of Pangloss! I rubbed my eyes, I looked at him attentively, I saw him hung; I fainted. Scarcely had I recovered my senses than I saw you stripped, stark naked, and this was the height of my horror, consternation, grief, and despair. I tell you, truthfully, that your skin is yet whiter and of a more perfect colour than that of my Bulgarian captain. This spectacle redoubled all the feelings which overwhelmed and devoured me. I screamed out, and would have said, 'Stop, barbarians!' but my voice failed me, and my cries would have been useless after you had been severely whipped. How is it possible, said I, that the beloved Candide and the wise Pangloss should both be at Lisbon, the one to receive a hundred lashes, and the other to be hanged by the Grand Inquisitor, of whom I am the well-beloved? Pangloss most cruelly deceived me when he said that everything in the world is for the best."

"Agitated, lost, sometimes beside myself, and sometimes ready to die of weakness, my mind was filled with the massacre of my father, mother, and brother, with the insolence of the ugly Bulgarian soldier, with the stab that he gave me, with my servitude under the Bulgarian captain, with my hideous Don Issachar, with my abominable Inquisitor, with the execution of Doctor Pangloss, with the grand Miserere to which they whipped you, and especially with the kiss I gave you behind the screen the day that I had last seen you. I praised God for bringing you back to me after so many trials, and I charged my old woman to take care of you, and to conduct you hither as soon as possible. She has executed her commission perfectly well; I have tasted the inexpressible pleasure of seeing you again, of hearing you, of speaking with you. But you must be hungry, for myself, I am famished; let us have supper."

They both sat down to table, and, when supper was over, they placed themselves once more on the sofa; where they were when Signor Don Issachar arrived. It was the Jewish Sabbath, and Issachar had come to enjoy his rights, and to explain his tender love.

WHAT BECAME OF CUNEGONDE, CANDIDE, THE GRAND INQUISITOR, AND THE JEW

This Issachar was the most choleric Hebrew that had ever been seen in Israel since the captivity in Babylon.

"What!" said he, "Thou bitch of a Galilean, was not the Inquisitor enough for thee? Must this rascal also share with me?"

In saying this he drew a long poniard which he always carried about him; and not imagining that his adversary had any arms he threw himself upon Candide: but our honest Westphalian had received a handsome sword from the old woman along with the suit of clothes. He drew his rapier, despite his gentleness, and laid the Israelite stone dead upon the cushions at Cunegonde's feet.

"Holy Virgin!" cried she, "what will become of us? A man killed in my apartment! If the officers of justice come, we are lost!"

"Had not Pangloss been hanged," said Candide, "he would give us good counsel in this emergency, for he was a profound philosopher. Failing him let us consult the old woman."

She was very prudent and commenced to give her opinion when suddenly another little door opened. It was an hour after midnight, it was the beginning of Sunday. This day belonged to my lord the Inquisitor. He entered, and saw the whipped Candide, sword in hand, a dead man upon the floor, Cunegonde aghast, and the old woman giving counsel. At this moment, the following is what passed in the soul of Candide, and how he reasoned:

If this holy man calls in assistance, he will surely have me burnt; and Cunegonde will perhaps be served in the same manner; he was the cause of my being cruelly whipped; he is my rival; and, as I have now begun to kill, I will kill away, for there is no time to hesitate.

This reasoning was clear and instantaneous; so that without giving time to the Inquisitor to recover from his surprise, he pierced him through and through, and cast him beside the Jew.

"Yet again!" said Cunegonde, "now there is no mercy for us, we are excommunicated, our last hour has come. How could you do it? you, naturally so gentle, to slay a Jew and a prelate in two minutes!"

"My beautiful young lady," responded Candide, "when one is a lover, jealous and whipped by the Inquisition, one stops at nothing."

The old woman then put in her word, saying:

"There are three Andalusian horses in the stable with bridles and saddles, let the brave Candide get them ready; madame has money, jewels; let us therefore mount quickly on horseback, though I can sit only on one buttock; let us set out for Cadiz, it is the finest weather in the world, and there is great pleasure in travelling in the cool of the night."

Immediately Candide saddled the three horses, and Cunegonde, the old woman and he, travelled thirty miles at a stretch.

While they were journeying, the Holy Brotherhood entered the house; the lord Inquisitor was interred in a handsome church, and Issachar's body was thrown upon a dunghill.

Candide, Cunegonde, and the old woman, had now reached the little town of Avacena in the midst of the mountains of the Sierra Morena, and were speaking as follows in a public inn.

IN WHAT DISTRESS CANDIDE, CUNEGONDE, AND THE OLD WOMAN ARRIVED AT CADIZ; AND OF THEIR EMBARKATION

"Who was it that robbed me of my money and jewels?" said Cunegonde, all bathed in tears. "How shall we live? What shall we do? Where find Inquisitors or Jews who will give me more?"

"Alas!" said the old woman, "I have a shrewd suspicion of a reverend Grey Friar, who stayed last night in the same inn with us at Badajos. God preserve me from judging rashly, but he came into our room twice, and he set out upon his journey long before us."

"Alas!" said Candide, "Dear Pangloss has often demonstrated to me that the goods of this world are common to all men, and that each has an equal right to them. But according to these principles the Grey Friar ought to have left us enough to carry us through our journey. Have you nothing at all left, my dear Cunegonde?"

"Not a farthing," said she.

"What then must we do?" said Candide.

"Sell one of the horses," replied the old woman. "I will ride behind Miss Cunegonde, though I can hold myself only on one buttock, and we shall reach Cadiz."

In the same inn there was a Benedictine prior who bought the horse for a cheap price. Candide, Cunegonde, and the old woman, having passed through Lucena, Chillas, and Lebrixa, arrived at length at Cadiz. A fleet was there getting ready, and troops assembling to bring to reason the reverend Jesuit Fathers of Paraguay, accused of having made one of the native tribes in the neighborhood of San Sacrament revolt against the Kings of Spain and Portugal. Candide having been in the Bulgarian service, performed the military exercise before the general of this little army with so graceful an address, with so intrepid an air, and with such agility and expedition, that he was given the command of a company of foot. Now, he was a captain! He set sail with Miss Cunegonde, the old woman, two valets, and the two Andalusian horses, which had belonged to the grand Inquisitor of Portugal.

During their voyage they reasoned a good deal on the philosophy of poor Pangloss.

"We are going into another world," said Candide; "and surely it must be there that all is for the best. For I must confess there is reason to complain a little of what passeth in our world in regard to both natural and moral philosophy."

"I love you with all my heart," said Cunegonde; "but my soul is still full of fright at that which I have seen and experienced."

"All will be well," replied Candide; "the sea of this new world is already better than our European sea; it is calmer, the winds more regular. It is certainly the New World which is the best of all possible worlds."

"God grant it," said Cunegonde; "but I have been so horribly unhappy there that my heart is almost closed to hope."

"You complain" said the old woman; "Alas! You have not known such misfortunes as mine."

Cunegonde almost broke out laughing, finding the good woman very amusing, for pretending to have been as unfortunate as she.

"Alas!" said Cunegonde, "My good mother, unless you have been ravished by two Bulgarians, have received two deep wounds in your belly, have had two castles demolished, have had two mothers cut to pieces before your eyes, and two of your lovers whipped at an auto-da-fé, I do not conceive how you could be more unfortunate than I. Add that I was born a baroness of seventy-two quarterings—and have been a cook!"

"Miss," replied the old woman, "you do not know my birth; and were I to show you my backside, you would not talk in that manner, but would suspend your judgment."

This speech having raised extreme curiosity in the minds of Cunegonde and Candide, the old woman spoke to them as follows.

HISTORY OF THE OLD WOMAN

"I had not always bleared eyes and red eyelids; neither did my nose always touch my chin; nor was I always a servant. I am the daughter of Pope Urban X, and of the Princess of Palestrina. Until the age of fourteen I was brought up in a palace, to which all the castles of your German barons would scarcely have served for stables; and one of my robes was worth more than all the magnificence of Westphalia. As I grew up I improved in beauty, wit, and every graceful accomplishment, in the midst of pleasures, hopes, and respectful homage. Already I inspired love. My throat was formed, and such a throat! White, firm, and shaped like that of the Venus of Medici; and what eyes! What eyelids! What black eyebrows! Such flames darted from my dark pupils that they eclipsed the scintillation of the stars—as I was told by the poets in our part of the world. My waiting women, when dressing and undressing me, used to fall into an ecstasy, whether they viewed me before or behind; how glad would the gentlemen have been to perform that office for them!"

"I was affianced to the most excellent Prince of Massa

Carara. Such a prince! As handsome as myself, sweet-tempered, agreeable, brilliantly witty, and sparkling with love. I loved him as one loves for the first time—with idolatry, with transport. The nuptials were prepared. There was surprising pomp and magnificence; there were fêtes, carousals, continual opera bouffe; and all Italy composed sonnets in my praise, though not one of them was passable. I was just upon the point of reaching the summit of bliss, when an old marchioness who had been mistress to the Prince, my husband, invited him to drink chocolate with her. He died in less than two hours of most terrible convulsions. But this is only a bagatelle. My mother, in despair, and scarcely less afflicted than myself, determined to absent herself for some time from so fatal a place. She had a very fine estate in the neighbourhood of Gaeta. We embarked on board a galley of the country which was gilded like the great altar of St. Peter's at Rome. A Sallee corsair swooped down and boarded us. Our men defended themselves like the Pope's soldiers; they flung themselves upon their knees, and threw down their arms, begging of the corsair an absolution in articulo mortis.

"Instantly they were stripped as bare as monkeys; my mother, our maids of honour, and myself were all served in the same manner. It is amazing with what expedition those gentry undress people. But what surprised me most was, that they thrust their fingers into the part of our bodies which the generality of women suffer no other instrument but—pipes to enter. It appeared to me a very strange kind of ceremony; but thus one judges of things when one has not seen the world. I afterwards learnt that it was to try whether we had concealed any diamonds. This is the practice established from time immemorial, among civilised nations that scour the seas. I was informed that the very religious Knights of Malta never fail to make this search when they take any Turkish prisoners of either sex. It is a law of nations from which they never deviate."

"I need not tell you how great a hardship it was for a young princess and her mother to be made slaves and carried to Morocco. You may easily imagine all we had to suffer on board the pirate vessel. My mother was still very handsome; our maids of honour, and even our waiting women, had more charms than are to be found in all Africa. As for myself, I was ravishing, was exquisite, grace itself, and I was a virgin! I did not remain so long; this flower, which had been reserved for the handsome Prince of Massa Carara, was plucked by the corsair captain. He was an abominable negro, and yet believed that he did me a great deal of honour. Certainly the Princess of Palestrina and myself must have been very strong to go through all that we experienced until our arrival at Morocco. But let us pass on; these are such common things as not to be worth mentioning."

"Morocco swam in blood when we arrived. Fifty sons of the Emperor Muley-Ismael had each their adherents; this produced fifty civil wars of blacks against blacks, and blacks against tawnies, and tawnies against tawnies, and mulattoes against mulattoes. In short it was a continual carnage throughout the empire."

"No sooner were we landed, than the blacks of a contrary faction to that of my captain attempted to rob him of his booty. Next to jewels and gold we were the most valuable things he had. I was witness to such a battle as you have never seen in your European climates. The northern nations have not that heat in their blood, nor that raging lust for women, so common in Africa. It seems that you Europeans have only milk in your veins; but it is vitriol, it is fire which runs in those of the inhabitants of Mount Atlas and the neighbouring countries. They fought with the fury of the lions, tigers, and serpents of the country, to see who should have us. A Moor seized my mother by the right arm, while my captain's lieutenant held her by the left; a Moorish soldier had hold of her by one leg, and one of our corsairs held her by the other. Thus almost all our women were drawn in quarters by four men. My captain concealed me behind him; and with his drawn scimitar cut and slashed every one that opposed his fury. At length I saw all our Italian women, and my mother herself, torn, mangled, massacred, by the monsters who disputed over them. The slaves, my companions, those who had taken them, soldiers, sailors, blacks, whites, mulattoes, and at last my captain, all were killed, and I remained dying on a heap of dead. Such scenes as this were transacted through an extent of three hundred leagues—and yet they never missed the five prayers a day ordained by Mahomet."

"With difficulty I disengaged myself from such a heap of slaughtered bodies, and crawled to a large orange tree on the bank of a neighbouring rivulet, where I fell, oppressed with fright, fatigue, horror, despair, and hunger. Immediately after, my senses, overpowered, gave themselves up to sleep, which was yet more swooning than repose. I was in this state of weakness and insensibility, between life and death, when I felt myself pressed by something that moved upon my body. I opened my eyes, and saw a white man, of good countenance, who sighed, and who said between his teeth: 'O che sciagura d'essere senza coglioni!'"

THE ADVENTURES OF THE
OLD WOMAN CONTINUED

"Astonished and delighted to hear my native language, and no less surprised at what this man said, I made answer that there were much greater misfortunes than that of which he complained. I told him in a few words of the horrors which I had endured, and fainted a second time. He carried me to a neighbouring house, put me to bed, gave me food, waited upon me, consoled me, flattered me; he told me that he had never seen any one so beautiful as I, and that he never so much regretted the loss of what it was impossible to recover."

"'I was born at Naples,' said he, 'there they geld two or three thousand children every year; some die of the operation, others acquire a voice more beautiful than that of women, and others are raised to offices of state. This operation was performed on me with great success and I was chapel musician to madam, the Princess of Palestrina.'"

"'To my mother!' cried I."

"'Your mother!' cried he, weeping. 'What! can you be that

young princess whom I brought up until the age of six years, and who promised so early to be as beautiful as you?'"

"'It is I, indeed; but my mother lies four hundred yards hence, torn in quarters, under a heap of dead bodies.'"

"I told him all my adventures, and he made me acquainted with his; telling me that he had been sent to the Emperor of Morocco by a Christian power, to conclude a treaty with that prince, in consequence of which he was to be furnished with military stores and ships to help to demolish the commerce of other Christian Governments."

"'My mission is done,' said this honest eunuch; 'I go to embark for Ceuta, and will take you to Italy. Ma che sciagura d'essere senza coglioni!'"

"I thanked him with tears of commiseration; and instead of taking me to Italy he conducted me to Algiers, where he sold me to the Dey. Scarcely was I sold, than the plague which had made the tour of Africa, Asia, and Europe, broke out with great malignancy in Algiers. You have seen earthquakes; but pray, miss, have you ever had the plague?"

"Never," answered Cunegonde.

"If you had," said the old woman, "you would acknowledge that it is far more terrible than an earthquake. It is common in Africa, and I caught it. Imagine to yourself the distressed situation of the daughter of a Pope, only fifteen years old, who, in less than three months, had felt the miseries of poverty and slavery, had been ravished almost every day, had beheld her mother drawn in quarters, had experienced famine and war, and was dying of the plague in Algiers. I did not die, however, but my eunuch, and the Dey, and almost the whole seraglio of Algiers perished."

"As soon as the first fury of this terrible pestilence was over, a sale was made of the Dey's slaves; I was purchased by a merchant, and carried to Tunis; this man sold me to another merchant, who sold me again to another at Tripoli; from Tripoli I was sold to Alexandria, from Alexandria to Smyrna, and from Smyrna to Constantinople. At length I became the property of an Aga of the Janissaries, who was soon ordered away to the defence of Azof, then besieged by the Russians."

"The Aga, who was a very gallant man, took his whole seraglio with him, and lodged us in a small fort on the Palus Méotides, guarded by two eunuchs and twenty soldiers. The Turks killed prodigious numbers of the Russians, but the latter had their revenge. Azof was destroyed by fire, the inhabitants put to the sword, neither sex nor age was spared; until there remained only our little fort, and the enemy wanted to starve us out. The twenty Janissaries had sworn they would never surrender. The extremities of famine to which they were reduced, obliged them to eat our two eunuchs, for fear of violating their oath. And at the end of a few days they resolved also to devour the women.

"We had a very pious and humane Iman, who preached an excellent sermon, exhorting them not to kill us all at once."

"'Only cut off a buttock of each of those ladies,' said he, 'and you'll fare extremely well; if you must go to it again, there will be the same entertainment a few days hence; heaven will accept of so charitable an action, and send you relief.'"

"He had great eloquence; he persuaded them; we underwent this terrible operation. The Iman applied the same balsam to us, as he does to children after circumcision; and we all nearly died."

"Scarcely had the Janissaries finished the repast with which we had furnished them, than the Russians came in flat-bottomed boats; not a Janissary escaped. The Russians paid no attention to the condition we were in. There are French surgeons in all parts of the world; one of them who was very clever took us under his care—he cured us; and as long as I live

I shall remember that as soon as my wounds were healed he made proposals to me. He bid us all be of good cheer, telling us that the like had happened in many sieges, and that it was according to the laws of war."

"As soon as my companions could walk, they were obliged to set out for Moscow. I fell to the share of a Boyard who made me his gardener, and gave me twenty lashes a day. But this nobleman having in two years' time been broke upon the wheel along with thirty more Boyards for some broils at court, I profited by that event; I fled. I traversed all Russia; I was a long time an inn-holder's servant at Riga, the same at Rostock, at Vismar, at Leipzig, at Cassel, at Utrecht, at Leyden, at the Hague, at Rotterdam. I waxed old in misery and disgrace, having only one-half of my posterior, and always remembering I was a Pope's daughter. A hundred times I was upon the point of killing myself; but still I loved life. This ridiculous foible is perhaps one of our most fatal characteristics; for is there anything more absurd than to wish to carry continually a burden which one can always throw down? To detest existence and yet to cling to one's existence? In brief, to caress the serpent which devours us, till he has eaten our very heart?

"In the different countries which it has been my lot to traverse, and the numerous inns where I have been servant, I have taken notice of a vast number of people who held their own existence in abhorrence, and yet I never knew of more than eight who voluntarily put an end to their misery; three negroes, four Englishmen, and a German professor named Robek. I ended by being servant to the Jew, Don Issachar, who placed me near your presence, my fair lady. I am determined to share your fate, and have been much more affected with your misfortunes than with my own. I would never even have spoken to you of my misfortunes, had you not piqued me a little, and if it were not customary to tell stories on board a ship in order to pass away the time. In short, Miss Cunegonde, I have had experience, I know the world; therefore I advise you to divert yourself, and prevail upon each passenger to tell his story; and if there be one of them all, that has not cursed his life many a time, that has not frequently looked upon himself as the unhappiest of mortals, I give you leave to throw me headforemost into the sea."

HOW CANDIDE WAS FORCED AWAY FROM HIS FAIR CUNEGONDE AND THE OLD WOMAN

The beautiful Cunegonde having heard the old woman's history, paid her all the civilities due to a person of her rank and merit. She likewise accepted her proposal, and engaged all the passengers, one after the other, to relate their adventures; and then both she and Candide allowed that the old woman was in the right.

"It is a great pity," said Candide, "that the sage Pangloss was hanged contrary to custom at an auto-da-fé; he would tell us most amazing things in regard to the physical and moral evils that overspread earth and sea, and I should be able, with due respect, to make a few objections."

While each passenger was recounting his story, the ship made her way. They landed at Buenos Ayres. Cunegonde, Captain Candide, and the old woman, waited on the Governor, Don Fernando d'Ibaraa, y Figueora, y Mascarenes, y Lampourdos, y Souza. This nobleman had a stateliness becoming a person who bore so many names. He spoke to men with so noble a disdain, carried his nose so loftily, raised his voice so unmercifully, assumed so imperious an air, and stalked with such intolerable pride, that those who saluted him were strongly inclined to give him a good drubbing. Cunegonde appeared to him the most beautiful he had ever met. The first thing he did was to ask whether she was not the captain's wife. The manner in which he asked the question alarmed Candide; he durst not say she was his wife, because indeed she was not; neither durst he say she was his sister, because it was not so; and although this obliging lie had been formerly much in favour among the ancients, and although it could be useful to the moderns, his soul was too pure to betray the truth."

"Miss Cunegonde," said he, "is to do me the honour to marry me, and we beseech your excellency to deign to sanction our marriage."

Don Fernando d'Ibaraa, y Figueora, y Mascarenes, y Lampourdos, y Souza, turning up his moustachio, smiled mockingly, and ordered Captain Candide to go and review his company. Candide obeyed, and the Governor remained alone with Miss Cunegonde. He declared his passion, protesting he would marry her the next day in the face of the church, or otherwise, just as should be agreeable to herself. Cunegonde asked a quarter of an hour to consider of it, to consult the old woman, and to take her resolution.

The old woman spoke thus to Cunegonde:

"Miss, you have seventy-two quarterings, and not a farthing; it is now in your power to be wife to the greatest lord in South America, who has a very beautiful moustachio. Is it for you to pique yourself upon inviolable fidelity? You have been ravished by Bulgarians; a Jew and an Inquisitor have enjoyed your favours. Misfortune gives sufficient excuse. I own, that if I were in your place, I should have no scruple in marrying the Governor and in making the fortune of Captain Candide."

While the old woman spoke with all the prudence which age and experience gave, a small ship entered the port on board of which were an Alcalde and his alguazils, and this was what had happened.

As the old woman had shrewdly guessed, it was a Grey Friar who stole Cunegonde's money and jewels in the town of Badajos, when she and Candide were escaping. The Friar wanted to sell some of the diamonds to a jeweller; the jeweller knew them to be the Grand Inquisitor's. The Friar before he was hanged confessed he had stolen them. He described the persons, and the route they had taken. The flight of Cunegonde and Candide was already known. They were traced to Cadiz. A vessel was immediately sent in pursuit of them. The vessel was already in the port of Buenos Ayres. The report spread that the Alcalde was going to land, and that he was in pursuit of the murderers of my lord the Grand Inquisitor. The prudent old woman saw at once what was to be done.

"You cannot run away," said she to Cunegonde, "and you have nothing to fear, for it was not you that killed my lord; besides the Governor who loves you will not suffer you to be ill-treated; therefore stay."

She then ran immediately to Candide.

"Fly," said she, "or in an hour you will be burnt."

There was not a moment to lose; but how could he part from Cunegonde, and where could he flee for shelter?

HOW CANDIDE AND CACAMBO WERE RECEIVED BY THE JESUITS OF PARAGUAY

Candide had brought such a valet with him from Cadiz, as one often meets with on the coasts of Spain and in the American colonies. He was a quarter Spaniard, born of a mongrel in Tucuman; he had been singing-boy, sacristan, sailor, monk, peddler, soldier, and lackey. His name was Cacambo, and he loved his master, because his master was a very good man. He quickly saddled the two Andalusian horses.

"Come, master, let us follow the old woman's advice; let us start, and run without looking behind us."

Candide shed tears.

"Oh! My dear Cunegonde! Must I leave you just at a time when the Governor was going to sanction our nuptials? Cunegonde, brought to such a distance what will become of you?"

"She will do as well as she can," said Cacambo; "the women are never at a loss, God provides for them, let us run."

"Whither art thou carrying me? Where shall we go? What shall we do without Cunegonde?" said Candide.

"By St. James of Compostella," said Cacambo, "you were

going to fight against the Jesuits; let us go to fight for them; I know the road well, I'll conduct you to their kingdom, where they will be charmed to have a captain that understands the Bulgarian exercise. You'll make a prodigious fortune; if we cannot find our account in one world we shall in another. It is a great pleasure to see and do new things."

"You have before been in Paraguay, then?" said Candide.

"Ay, sure," answered Cacambo, "I was servant in the College of the Assumption, and am acquainted with the government of the good Fathers as well as I am with the streets of Cadiz. It is an admirable government. The kingdom is upwards of three hundred leagues in diameter, and divided into thirty provinces; there the Fathers possess all, and the people nothing; it is a masterpiece of reason and justice. For my part I see nothing so divine as the Fathers who here make war upon the kings of Spain and Portugal, and in Europe confess those kings; who here kill Spaniards, and in Madrid send them to heaven; this delights me, let us push forward. You are going to be the happiest of mortals. What pleasure will it be to those Fathers to hear that a captain who knows the Bulgarian exercise has come to them!"

As soon as they reached the first barrier, Cacambo told the advanced guard that a captain wanted to speak with my lord the Commandant. Notice was given to the main guard, and immediately a Paraguayan officer ran and laid himself at the feet of the Commandant, to impart this news to him. Candide and Cacambo were disarmed, and their two Andalusian horses seized. The strangers were introduced between two files of musketeers; the Commandant was at the further end, with the three-cornered cap on his head, his gown tucked up, a sword by his side, and a spontoon in his hand. He beckoned, and straightway the new-comers were encompassed by four-and-twenty soldiers. A sergeant told them they must wait, that the

Commandant could not speak to them, and that the reverend Father Provincial does not suffer any Spaniard to open his mouth but in his presence, or to stay above three hours in the province.

"And where is the reverend Father Provincial?" said Cacambo.

"He is upon the parade just after celebrating mass," answered the sergeant, "and you cannot kiss his spurs till three hours hence."

"However," said Cacambo, "the captain is not a Spaniard, but a German, he is ready to perish with hunger as well as myself; cannot we have something for breakfast, while we wait for his reverence?"

The sergeant went immediately to acquaint the Commandant with what he had heard.

"God be praised!" said the reverend Commandant, "Since he is a German, I may speak to him; take him to my arbour."

Candide was at once conducted to a beautiful summer-house, ornamented with a very pretty colonnade of green and gold marble, and with trellises, enclosing parraquets, humming-birds, fly-birds, guinea-hens, and all other rare birds. An excellent breakfast was provided in vessels of gold; and while the Paraguayans were eating maize out of wooden dishes, in the open fields and exposed to the heat of the sun, the reverend Father Commandant retired to his arbour.

He was a very handsome young man, with a full face, white skin but high in colour; he had an arched eyebrow, a lively eye, red ears, vermilion lips, a bold air, but such a boldness as neither belonged to a Spaniard nor a Jesuit. They returned their arms to Candide and Cacambo, and also the two Andalusian horses; to whom Cacambo gave some oats to eat just by the arbour, having an eye upon them all the while for fear of a surprise.

Candide first kissed the hem of the Commandant's robe, then they sat down to table.

"You are, then, a German?" said the Jesuit to him in that language.

"Yes, reverend Father," answered Candide.

As they pronounced these words they looked at each other with great amazement, and with such an emotion as they could not conceal.

"And from what part of Germany do you come?" said the Jesuit.

"I am from the dirty province of Westphalia," answered Candide; "I was born in the Castle of Thunder-ten-Tronckh."

"Oh! Heavens! is it possible?" cried the Commandant.

"What a miracle!" cried Candide.

"Is it really you?" said the Commandant.

"It is not possible!" said Candide.

They drew back; they embraced; they shed rivulets of tears.

"What, is it you, reverend Father? You, the brother of the fair Cunegonde! You, that was slain by the Bulgarians! You, the Baron's son! You, a Jesuit in Paraguay! I must confess this is a strange world that we live in. Oh, Pangloss! Pangloss! How glad you would be if you had not been hanged!"

The Commandant sent away the negro slaves and the Paraguayans, who served them with liquors in goblets of rock-crystal. He thanked God and St. Ignatius a thousand times; he clasped Candide in his arms; and their faces were all bathed with tears.

"You will be more surprised, more affected, and transport-ed," said Candide, "when I tell you that Cunegonde, your sister, whom you believe to have been ripped open, is in perfect health."

"Where?"

"In your neighbourhood, with the Governor of Buenos Ayres; and I was going to fight against you."

Every word which they uttered in this long conversation but added wonder to wonder. Their souls fluttered on their tongues, listened in their ears, and sparkled in their eyes. As they were Germans, they sat a good while at table, waiting for the reverend Father Provincial, and the Commandant spoke to his dear Candide as follows.

HOW CANDIDE KILLED
THE BROTHER OF HIS
DEAR CUNEGONDE

"I shall have ever present to my memory the dreadful day, on which I saw my father and mother killed, and my sister ravished. When the Bulgarians retired, my dear sister could not be found; but my mother, my father, and myself, with two maid-servants and three little boys all of whom had been slain, were put in a hearse, to be conveyed for interment to a chapel belonging to the Jesuits, within two leagues of our family seat. A Jesuit sprinkled us with some holy water; it was horribly salty; a few drops of it fell into my eyes; the father perceived that my eyelids stirred a little; he put his hand upon my heart and felt it beat. I received assistance, and at the end of three weeks I recovered. You know, my dear Candide, I was very pretty; but I grew much prettier, and the reverend Father Didrie, Superior of that House, conceived the tenderest friendship for me; he gave me the habit of the order, some years after I was sent to Rome. The Father-General needed new levies of young German-Jesuits. The sovereigns of Paraguay admit as few Spanish Jesuits as possible; they prefer those of other nations as being more subordinate to their commands. I was judged fit by the reverend Father-General to go and work in this vineyard. We set out—a Pole, a Tyrolese, and myself. Upon my arrival I was honoured with a sub-deaconship and a lieutenancy. I am today colonel and priest. We shall give a warm reception to the King of Spain's troops; I will answer for it that they shall be excommunicated and well beaten. Providence sends you here to assist us. But is it, indeed, true that my dear sister Cunegonde is in the neighbourhood, with the Governor of Buenos Ayres?"

Candide assured him on oath that nothing was more true, and their tears began afresh.

The Baron could not refrain from embracing Candide; he called him his brother, his saviour.

"Ah! perhaps," said he, "we shall together, my dear Candide, enter the town as conquerors, and recover my sister Cunegonde."

"That is all I want," said Candide, "for I intended to marry her, and I still hope to do so."

"You insolent!" replied the Baron, "Would you have the impudence to marry my sister who has seventy-two quarterings! I find thou hast the most consummate effrontery to dare to mention so presumptuous a design!"

Candide, petrified at this speech, made answer:

"Reverend Father, all the quarterings in the world signify nothing; I rescued your sister from the arms of a Jew and of an Inquisitor; she has great obligations to me, she wishes to marry me; Master Pangloss always told me that all men are equal, and certainly I will marry her."

"We shall see that, thou scoundrel!" said the Jesuit Baron de Thunder-ten-Tronckh, and that instant struck him across the face with the flat of his sword. Candide in an instant drew his rapier, and plunged it up to the hilt in the Jesuit's belly; but in pulling it out reeking hot, he burst into tears.

"Good God!" said he, "I have killed my old master, my friend, my brother-in-law! I am the best-natured creature in the world, and yet I have already killed three men, and of these three two were priests."

Cacambo, who stood sentry by the door of the arbour, ran to him.

"We have nothing more for it than to sell our lives as dearly as we can," said his master to him, "without doubt someone will soon enter the arbour, and we must die sword in hand."

Cacambo, who had been in a great many scrapes in his lifetime, did not lose his head; he took the Baron's Jesuit habit, put it on Candide, gave him the square cap, and made him mount on horseback. All this was done in the twinkling of an eye.

"Let us gallop fast, master, everybody will take you for a Jesuit, going to give directions to your men, and we shall have passed the frontiers before they will be able to overtake us."

He flew as he spoke these words, crying out aloud in Spanish:

"Make way, make way, for the reverend Father Colonel."

ADVENTURES OF THE TWO TRAVELLERS, WITH TWO GIRLS, TWO MONKEYS, AND THE SAVAGES CALLED OREILLONS

Candide and his valet had got beyond the barrier, before it was known in the camp that the German Jesuit was dead. The wary Cacambo had taken care to fill his wallet with bread, chocolate, bacon, fruit, and a few bottles of wine. With their Andalusian horses they penetrated into an unknown country, where they perceived no beaten track. At length they came to a beautiful meadow intersected with purling rills. Here our two adventurers fed their horses. Cacambo proposed to his master to take some food, and he set him an example.

"How can you ask me to eat ham," said Candide, "after killing the Baron's son, and being doomed never more to see the beautiful Cunegonde? What will it avail me to spin out my wretched days and drag them far from her in remorse and despair? And what will the Journal of Trevoux say?"

While he was thus lamenting his fate, he went on eating. The sun went down. The two wanderers heard some little cries which seemed to be uttered by women. They did not know whether they were cries of pain or joy; but they started up precipitately with that inquietude and alarm which every little thing inspires in an unknown country. The noise was made by two naked girls, who tripped along the mead, while two monkeys were pursuing them and biting their buttocks. Candide was moved with pity; he had learned to fire a gun in the Bulgarian service, and he was so clever at it, that he could hit a filbert in a hedge without touching a leaf of the tree. He took up his double-barrelled Spanish fusil, let it off, and killed the two monkeys.

"God be praised! My dear Cacambo, I have rescued those two poor creatures from a most perilous situation. If I have committed a sin in killing an Inquisitor and a Jesuit, I have made ample amends by saving the lives of these girls. Perhaps they are young ladies of family; and this adventure may procure us great advantages in this country."

He was continuing, but stopped short when he saw the two girls tenderly embracing the monkeys, bathing their bodies in tears, and rending the air with the most dismal lamentations.

"Little did I expect to see such good nature," said he at length to Cacambo; who made answer:

"Master, you have done a fine thing now; you have slain the sweethearts of those two young ladies."

"The sweethearts! Is it possible? You are jesting, Cacambo, I can never believe it!"

"Dear master," replied Cacambo; "you are surprised at everything. Why should you think it so strange that in some countries there are monkeys which insinuate themselves into the good graces of the ladies; they are a fourth part human, as I am a fourth part Spaniard."

"Alas!" replied Candide, "I remember to have heard Master Pangloss say, that formerly such accidents used to happen; that these mixtures were productive of Centaurs, Fauns, and Satyrs;

and that many of the ancients had seen such monsters, but I looked upon the whole as fabulous."

"You ought now to be convinced," said Cacambo, "that it is the truth, and you see what use is made of those creatures, by persons that have not had a proper education; all I fear is that those ladies will play us some ugly trick."

These sound reflections induced Candide to leave the meadow and to plunge into a wood. He supped there with Cacambo; and after cursing the Portuguese inquisitor, the Governor of Buenos Ayres, and the Baron, they fell asleep on moss. On awaking they felt that they could not move; for during the night the Oreillons, who inhabited that country, and to whom the ladies had denounced them, had bound them with cords made of the bark of trees. They were encompassed by fifty naked Oreillons, armed with bows and arrows, with clubs and flint hatchets. Some were making a large cauldron boil, others were preparing spits, and all cried:

"A Jesuit! a Jesuit! We shall be revenged, we shall have excellent cheer, let us eat the Jesuit, let us eat him up!"

"I told you, my dear master," cried Cacambo sadly, "that those two girls would play us some ugly trick."

Candide seeing the cauldron and the spits, cried:

"We are certainly going to be either roasted or boiled. Ah! What would Master Pangloss say, were he to see how pure nature is formed? Everything is right, may be, but I declare it is very hard to have lost Miss Cunegonde and to be put upon a spit by Oreillons."

Cacambo never lost his head.

"Do not despair," said he to the disconsolate Candide, "I understand a little of the jargon of these people, I will speak to them."

"Be sure," said Candide, "to represent to them how frightfully inhuman it is to cook men, and how very un-Christian."

"Gentlemen," said Cacambo, "you reckon you are today going to feast upon a Jesuit. It is all very well, nothing is more unjust than thus to treat your enemies. Indeed, the law of nature teaches us to kill our neighbour, and such is the practice all over the world. If we do not accustom ourselves to eating them, it is because we have better fare. But you have not the same resources as we; certainly it is much better to devour your enemies than to resign to the crows and rooks the fruits of your victory. But, gentlemen, surely you would not choose to eat your friends. You believe that you are going to spit a Jesuit, and he is your defender. It is the enemy of your enemies that you are going to roast. As for myself, I was born in your country; this gentleman is my master, and, far from being a Jesuit, he has just killed one, whose spoils he wears; and thence comes your mistake. To convince you of the truth of what I say, take his habit and carry it to the first barrier of the Jesuit kingdom, and inform yourselves whether my master did not kill a Jesuit officer. It will not take you long, and you can always eat us if you find that I have lied to you. But I have told you the truth. You are too well acquainted with the principles of public law, humanity, and justice not to pardon us."

The Oreillons found this speech very reasonable. They deputed two of their principal people with all expedition to inquire into the truth of the matter; these executed their commission like men of sense, and soon returned with good news. The Oreillons untied their prisoners, showed them all sorts of civilities, offered them girls, gave them refreshment, and reconducted them to the confines of their territories, proclaiming with great joy:

"He is no Jesuit! He is no Jesuit!"

Candide could not help being surprised at the cause of his deliverance.

"What people!" said he; "What men! What manners! If I

had not been so lucky as to run Miss Cunegonde's brother through the body, I should have been devoured without redemption. But, after all, pure nature is good, since these people, instead of feasting upon my flesh, have shown me a thousand civilities, when then I was not a Jesuit."

ARRIVAL OF CANDIDE AND
HIS VALET AT EL DORADO,
AND WHAT THEY SAW THERE

"You see," said Cacambo to Candide, as soon as they had reached the frontiers of the Oreillons, "that this hemisphere is not better than the others, take my word for it; let us go back to Europe by the shortest way."

"How do we go back?" said Candide, "And where shall we go? To my own country? The Bulgarians and the Abares are slaying all; to Portugal? There I shall be burnt; and if we abide here we are every moment in danger of being spitted. But how can I resolve to quit a part of the world where my dear Cunegonde resides?"

"Let us turn towards Cayenne," said Cacambo, "there we shall find Frenchmen, who wander all over the world; they may assist us; God will perhaps have pity on us."

It was not easy to get to Cayenne; they knew vaguely in which direction to go, but rivers, precipices, robbers, savages, obstructed them all the way. Their horses died of fatigue. Their provisions were consumed; they fed a whole month upon wild fruits, and found themselves at last near a little river bordered with cocoa trees, which sustained their lives and their hopes.

Cacambo, who was as good a counsellor as the old woman, said to Candide:

"We are able to hold out no longer; we have walked enough. I see an empty canoe near the river-side; let us fill it with cocoanuts, throw ourselves into it, and go with the current; a river always leads to some inhabited spot. If we do not find pleasant things we shall at least find new things."

"With all my heart," said Candide, "let us recommend ourselves to Providence."

They rowed a few leagues, between banks, in some places flowery, in others barren; in some parts smooth, in others rugged. The stream ever widened, and at length lost itself under an arch of frightful rocks which reached to the sky. The two travellers had the courage to commit themselves to the current. The river, suddenly contracting at this place, whirled them along with a dreadful noise and rapidity. At the end of four-and-twenty hours they saw daylight again, but their canoe was dashed to pieces against the rocks. For a league they had to creep from rock to rock, until at length they discovered an extensive plain, bounded by inaccessible mountains. The country was cultivated as much for pleasure as for necessity. On all sides the useful was also the beautiful. The roads were covered, or rather adorned, with carriages of a glittering form and substance, in which were men and women of surprising beauty, drawn by large red sheep which surpassed in fleetness the finest coursers of Andalusia, Tetuan, and Mequinez.

"Here, however, is a country," said Candide, "which is better than Westphalia."

He stepped out with Cacambo towards the first village which he saw. Some children dressed in tattered brocades played at quoits on the outskirts. Our travellers from the other world amused themselves by looking on. The quoits were large round pieces, yellow, red, and green, which cast a singular lustre. The travellers picked a few of them off the ground; this was of gold, that of emeralds, the other of rubies—the least of them would have been the greatest ornament on the Mogul's throne.

"Without doubt," said Cacambo, "these children must be the king's sons that are playing at quoits!"

The village schoolmaster appeared at this moment and called them to school.

"There," said Candide, "is the preceptor of the royal family."

The little truants immediately quitted their game, leaving the quoits on the ground with all their other playthings. Candide gathered them up, ran to the master, and presented them to him in a most humble manner, giving him to understand by signs that their royal highnesses had forgotten their gold and jewels. The schoolmaster, smiling, flung them upon the ground; then, looking at Candide with a good deal of surprise, went about his business.

The travellers, however, took care to gather up the gold, the rubies, and the emeralds.

"Where are we?" cried Candide. "The king's children in this country must be well brought up, since they are taught to despise gold and precious stones."

Cacambo was as much surprised as Candide. At length they drew near the first house in the village. It was built like a European palace. A crowd of people pressed about the door, and there were still more in the house. They heard most agreeable music, and were aware of a delicious odour of cooking. Cacambo went up to the door and heard they were talking Peruvian; it was his mother tongue, for it is well known that Cacambo was born in Tucuman, in a village where no other language was spoken.

"I will be your interpreter here," said he to Candide; "let us go in, it is a public-house."

Immediately two waiters and two girls, dressed in cloth of gold, and their hair tied up with ribbons, invited them to sit down to table with the landlord. They served four dishes of soup, each garnished with two young parrots; a boiled condor which weighed two hundred pounds; two roasted monkeys, of excellent flavour; three hundred humming-birds in one dish, and six hundred fly-birds in another; exquisite ragouts; delicious pastries; the whole served up in dishes of a kind of rock-crystal. The waiters and girls poured out several liqueurs drawn from the sugar cane.

Most of the company were chapmen and waggoners, all extremely polite; they asked Cacambo a few questions with the greatest circumspection, and answered his in the most obliging manner.

As soon as dinner was over, Cacambo believed as well as Candide that they might well pay their reckoning by laying down two of those large gold pieces which they had picked up. The landlord and landlady shouted with laughter and held their sides. When the fit was over:

"Gentlemen," said the landlord, "it is plain you are strangers, and such guests we are not accustomed to see; pardon us therefore for laughing when you offered us the pebbles from our highroads in payment of your reckoning. You doubtless have not the money of the country; but it is not necessary to have any money at all to dine in this house. All hostelries established for the convenience of commerce are paid by the government. You have fared but very indifferently because this is a poor village; but everywhere else, you will be received as you deserve."

Cacambo explained this whole discourse with great astonishment to Candide, who was as greatly astonished to hear it.

"What sort of a country then is this," said they to one another; "a country unknown to all the rest of the world, and where nature is of a kind so different from ours? It is probably the country where all is well; for there absolutely must be one such place. And, whatever Master Pangloss might say, I often found that things went very ill in Westphalia."

WHAT THEY SAW IN THE COUNTRY OF EL DORADO

Cacambo expressed his curiosity to the landlord, who made answer:

"I am very ignorant, but not the worse on that account. However, we have in this neighbourhood an old man retired from Court who is the most learned and most communicative person in the kingdom."

At once he took Cacambo to the old man. Candide acted now only a second character, and accompanied his valet. They entered a very plain house, for the door was only of silver, and the ceilings were only of gold, but wrought in so elegant a taste as to vie with the richest. The antechamber, indeed, was only encrusted with rubies and emeralds, but the order in which everything was arranged made amends for this great simplicity.

The old man received the strangers on his sofa, which was stuffed with humming-birds' feathers, and ordered his servants to present them with liqueurs in diamond goblets; after which he satisfied their curiosity in the following terms:

"I am now one hundred and seventy-two years old, and I learnt of my late father, Master of the Horse to the King, the amazing revolutions of Peru, of which he had been an eyewitness. The kingdom we now inhabit is the ancient country of the Incas, who quitted it very imprudently to conquer another part of the world, and were at length destroyed by the Spaniards."

"More wise by far were the princes of their family, who remained in their native country; and they ordained, with the consent of the whole nation, that none of the inhabitants should ever be permitted to quit this little kingdom; and this has preserved our innocence and happiness. The Spaniards have had a confused notion of this country, and have called it El Dorado; and an Englishman, whose name was Sir Walter Raleigh, came very near it about a hundred years ago; but being surrounded by inaccessible rocks and precipices, we have hitherto been sheltered from the rapaciousness of European nations, who have an inconceivable passion for the pebbles and dirt of our land, for the sake of which they would murder us to the last man."

The conversation was long: it turned chiefly on their form of government, their manners, their women, their public entertainments, and the arts. At length Candide, having always had a taste for metaphysics, made Cacambo ask whether there was any religion in that country.

The old man reddened a little.

"How then," said he, "can you doubt it? Do you take us for ungrateful wretches?"

Cacambo humbly asked, "What was the religion in El Dorado?"

The old man reddened again.

"Can there be two religions?" said he. "We have, I believe, the religion of all the world: we worship God night and morning."

"Do you worship but one God?" said Cacambo, who still acted as interpreter in representing Candide's doubts.

"Surely," said the old man, "there are not two, nor three, nor four. I must confess the people from your side of the world ask very extraordinary questions."

Candide was not yet tired of interrogating the good old man; he wanted to know in what manner they prayed to God in El Dorado.

"We do not pray to Him," said the worthy sage; "we have nothing to ask of Him; He has given us all we need, and we return Him thanks without ceasing."

Candide having a curiosity to see the priests asked where they were.

The good old man smiled.

"My friend," said he, "we are all priests. The King and all the heads of families sing solemn canticles of thanksgiving every morning, accompanied by five or six thousand musicians."

"What! have you no monks who teach, who dispute, who govern, who cabal, and who burn people that are not of their opinion?"

"We must be mad, indeed, if that were the case," said the old man; "here we are all of one opinion, and we know not what you mean by monks."

During this whole discourse Candide was in raptures, and he said to himself, "This is vastly different from Westphalia and the Baron's castle. Had our friend Pangloss seen El Dorado he would no longer have said that the castle of Thunder-ten-Tronckh was the finest upon earth. It is evident that one must travel."

After this long conversation the old man ordered a coach and six sheep to be got ready, and twelve of his domestics to conduct the travelers to Court.

"Excuse me," said he, "if my age deprives me of the honour of accompanying you. The King will receive you in a manner that cannot displease you; and no doubt you will make an allowance for the customs of the country, if some things should not be to your liking."

Candide and Cacambo got into the coach, the six sheep flew, and in less than four hours they reached the King's palace situated at the extremity of the capital. The portal was two-hundred and twenty feet high, and one-hundred wide; but words are wanting to express the materials of which it was built. It is plain such materials must have prodigious superiority over those pebbles and sand which we call gold and precious stones.

Twenty beautiful damsels of the King's guard received Candide and Cacambo as they alighted from the coach, conducted them to the bath, and dressed them in robes woven of the down of hummingbirds; after which the great crown officers, of both sexes, led them to the King's apartment, between two files of musicians, a thousand on each side. When they drew near to the audience chamber Cacambo asked one of the great officers in what way he should pay his obeisance to his Majesty; whether they should throw themselves upon their knees or on their stomachs; whether they should put their hands upon their heads or behind their backs; whether they should lick the dust off the floor; in a word, what was the ceremony?

"The custom," said the great officer, "is to embrace the King, and to kiss him on each cheek."

Candide and Cacambo threw themselves round his Majesty's neck. He received them with all the goodness imaginable, and politely invited them to supper.

While waiting they were shown the city, and saw the public edifices raised as high as the clouds, the market places ornamented with a thousand columns, the fountains of spring water, those of rose water, those of liqueurs drawn from sugar-cane, incessantly flowing into the great squares, which were paved with a kind of precious stone, which gave off a delicious fragrancy like that of cloves and cinnamon. Candide asked to see the court of justice, the parliament. They told him they had none, and that they were strangers to lawsuits. He asked if they had any prisons, and they answered no. But what surprised him most and gave him the greatest pleasure was the palace of sciences, where he saw a gallery two thousand feet long, and filled with instruments employed in mathematics and physics.

After rambling about the city the whole afternoon, and seeing but a thousandth part of it, they were reconducted to the royal palace, where Candide sat down to table with his Majesty, his valet Cacambo, and several ladies. Never was there a better entertainment, and never was more wit shown at a table than that which fell from his Majesty. Cacambo explained the King's bon-mots to Candide, and notwithstanding they were translated they still appeared to be bon-mots. Of all the things that surprised Candide this was not the least.

They spent a month in this hospitable place. Candide frequently said to Cacambo:

"I own, my friend, once more that the castle where I was born is nothing in comparison with this; but, after all, Miss Cunegonde is not here, and you have, without doubt, some mistress in Europe. If we abide here we shall only be upon a footing with the rest, whereas, if we return to our old world, only with twelve sheep laden with the pebbles of El Dorado, we shall be richer than all the kings in Europe. We shall have no more Inquisitors to fear, and we may easily recover Miss Cunegonde."

This speech was agreeable to Cacambo; mankind people are so fond of roving, of making a figure in their own country, and of boasting of what they have seen in their travels, that the two happy ones resolved to be no longer so, but to ask his Majesty's leave to quit the country.

"You are foolish," said the King. "I am sensible that my kingdom is but a small place, but when a person is comfortably settled in any part, he should abide there. I have not the right to detain strangers. It is a tyranny which neither our manners nor our laws permit. All men are free. Go when you wish, but the going will be very difficult. It is impossible to ascend that rapid river on which you came as by a miracle, and which runs under vaulted rocks. The mountains which surround my kingdom are ten thousand feet high, and as steep as walls; they are each over ten leagues in breadth, and there is no other way to descend them than by precipices. However, since you absolutely wish to depart, I shall give orders to my engineers to construct a machine that will convey you very safely. When we have conducted you over the mountains no one can accompany you further, for my subjects have made a vow never to quit the kingdom, and they are too wise to break it. Ask me besides anything that you please."

"We desire nothing of your Majesty," says Candide, "but a few sheep laden with provisions, pebbles, and the earth of this country."

The King laughed.

"I cannot conceive," said he, "what pleasure you Europeans find in our yellow clay, but take as much as you like, and great good may it do you."

At once he gave directions that his engineers should construct a machine to hoist up these two extraordinary men out of the kingdom. Three thousand good mathematicians went to work; it was ready in fifteen days, and did not cost more than twenty million sterling in the specie of that country. They placed Candide and Cacambo on the machine. There were two great red sheep saddled and bridled to ride upon as soon as they were beyond the mountains, twenty pack-sheep laden with provisions, thirty with presents of the curiosities of the country, and fifty with gold, diamonds, and precious stones. The King embraced the two wanderers very tenderly.

Their departure, with the ingenious manner in which they and their sheep were hoisted over the mountains, was a splendid spectacle. The mathematicians took their leave after conveying them to a place of safety, and Candide had no other desire, no other aim, than to present his sheep to Miss Cunegonde.

"Now," said he, "we are able to pay the Governor of Buenos Ayres if Miss Cunegonde can be ransomed. Let us journey towards Cayenne. Let us embark, and we will afterwards see what kingdom we shall be able to purchase."

WHAT HAPPENED TO THEM AT SURINAM AND HOW CANDIDE GOT ACQUAINTED WITH MARTIN

Our travellers spent the first day very agreeably. They were delighted with possessing more treasure than all Asia, Europe, and Africa could scrape together. Candide, in his raptures, cut Cunegonde's name on the trees. The second day two of their sheep plunged into a morass, where they and their burdens were lost; two more died of fatigue a few days after; seven or eight perished with hunger in a desert; and others subsequently fell down precipices. At length, after travelling a hundred days, only two sheep remained.

Said Candide to Cacambo, "My friend, you see how perishable are the riches of this world; there is nothing solid but virtue, and the happiness of seeing Cunegonde once more."

"I grant all you say," said Cacambo, "but we have still two sheep remaining, with more treasure than the King of Spain will ever have; and I see a town which I take to be Surinam, belonging to the Dutch. We are at the end of all our troubles, and at the beginning of happiness."

As they drew near the town, they saw a negro stretched

upon the ground, with only one moiety of his clothes, that is, of his blue linen drawers; the poor man had lost his left leg and his right hand.

"Good God!" said Candide in Dutch, "what art thou doing there, friend, in that shocking condition?"

"I am waiting for my master, Mynheer Vanderdendur, the famous merchant," answered the negro.

"Was it Mynheer Vanderdendur," said Candide, "that treated thee thus?"

"Yes, sir," said the negro, "it is the custom. They give us a pair of linen drawers for our whole garment twice a year. When we work at the sugarcanes, and the mill snatches hold of a finger, they cut off the hand; and when we attempt to run away, they cut off the leg; both cases have happened to me. This is the price at which you eat sugar in Europe. Yet when my mother sold me for ten patagons on the coast of Guinea, she said to me: 'My dear child, bless our fetiches, adore them forever; they will make thee live happily; thou hast the honour of being the slave of our lords, the whites, which is making the fortune of thy father and mother.' Alas! I know not whether I have made their fortunes; this I know, that they have not made mine. Dogs, monkeys, and parrots are a thousand times less wretched than I. The Dutch fetiches, who have converted me, declare every Sunday that we are all of us children of Adam—blacks as well as whites. I am not a genealogist, but if these preachers tell truth, we are all second cousins. Now, you must agree, that it is impossible to treat one's relations in a more barbarous manner."

"Oh, Pangloss!" cried Candide, "you had not guessed at this abomination; it is the end. I must at last renounce your optimism."

"What is this optimism?" said Cacambo.

"Alas!" said Candide, "it is the madness of maintaining that everything is right when it is wrong."

Looking at the negro, he shed tears, and weeping, he entered Surinam.

The first thing they inquired after was whether there was a vessel in the harbour which could be sent to Buenos Ayres. The person to whom they applied was a Spanish sea captain, who offered to agree with them upon reasonable terms. He appointed to meet them at a public-house, whither Candide and the faithful Cacambo went with their two sheep, and awaited his coming.

Candide, who had his heart upon his lips, told the Spaniard all his adventures, and avowed that he intended to elope with Miss Cunegonde.

"Then I will take good care not to carry you to Buenos Ayres," said the seaman. "I should be hanged, and so would you. The fair Cunegonde is my lord's favourite mistress."

This was a thunderclap for Candide: he wept for a long while. At last he drew Cacambo aside.

"Here, my dear friend," said he to him, "this thou must do. We have, each of us in his pocket, five or six millions in diamonds; you are more clever than I; you must go and bring Miss Cunegonde from Buenos Ayres. If the Governor makes any difficulty, give him a million; if he will not relinquish her, give him two; as you have not killed an Inquisitor, they will have no suspicion of you; I'll get another ship, and go and wait for you at Venice; that's a free country, where there is no danger either from Bulgarians, Abares, Jews, or Inquisitors."

Cacambo applauded this wise resolution. He despaired at parting from so good a master, who had become his intimate friend; but the pleasure of serving him prevailed over the pain of leaving him. They embraced with tears; Candide charged him not to forget the good old woman. Cacambo set out that very same day. This Cacambo was a very honest fellow.

Candide stayed some time longer in Surinam, waiting for another captain to carry him and the two remaining sheep to Italy. After he had hired domestics, and purchased everything necessary for a long voyage, Mynheer Vanderdendur, captain of a large vessel, came and offered his services.

"How much will you charge," said he to this man, "to carry me straight to Venice—me, my servants, my baggage, and these two sheep?"

The skipper asked ten thousand piastres. Candide did not hesitate.

"Oh! oh!" said the prudent Vanderdendur to himself, "this stranger gives ten thousand piastres unhesitatingly! He must be very rich."

Returning a little while after, he let him know that upon second consideration, he could not undertake the voyage for less than twenty thousand piastres.

"Well, you shall have them." said Candide.

"Ay!" said the skipper to himself, "this man agrees to pay twenty thousand piastres with as much ease as ten."

He went back to him again, and declared that he could not carry him to Venice for less than thirty thousand piastres.

"Then you shall have thirty thousand." replied Candide.

"Oh! oh!" said the Dutch skipper once more to himself, "thirty thousand piastres are a trifle to this man; surely these sheep must be laden with an immense treasure; let us say no more about it. First of all, let him pay down the thirty thousand piastres; then we shall see."

Candide sold two small diamonds, the least of which was worth more than what the skipper asked for his freight. He paid him in advance. The two sheep were put on board. Candide followed in a little boat to join the vessel in the roads. The skipper seized his opportunity, set sail, and put out to sea, the wind favouring him. Candide, dismayed and stupefied, soon lost sight of the vessel.

"Alas!" said he, "this is a trick worthy of the old world!"

He put back, overwhelmed with sorrow, for indeed he had lost sufficient to make the fortune of twenty monarchs. He waited upon the Dutch magistrate, and in his distress, he knocked over-loudly at the door. He entered and told his adventure, raising his voice with unnecessary vehemence. The magistrate began by fining him ten thousand piastres for making a noise; then he listened patiently, promised to examine into his affair at the skipper's return, and ordered him to pay ten thousand piastres for the expense of the hearing.

This drove Candide to despair; he had, indeed, endured misfortunes a thousand times worse; the coolness of the magistrate and of the skipper who had robbed him, roused his choler and flung him into a deep melancholy. The villainy of mankind presented itself before his imagination in all its deformity, and his mind was filled with gloomy ideas. At length hearing that a French vessel was ready to set sail for Bordeaux, as he had no sheep laden with diamonds to take along with him he hired a cabin at the usual price. He made it known in the town that he would pay the passage and board and give two thousand piastres to any honest man who would make the voyage with him, upon condition that this man was the most dissatisfied with his state, and the most unfortunate in the whole province.

Such a crowd of candidates presented themselves that a fleet of ships could hardly have held them. Candide being desirous of selecting from among the best, marked out about one-twentieth of them who seemed to be sociable men, and who all pretended to merit his preference. He assembled them at his inn, and gave them a supper on condition that each took an oath to relate his history faithfully, promising to choose him who appeared to be most justly discontented with his state, and to bestow some presents upon the rest.

They sat until four o'clock in the morning. Candide, in listening to all their adventures, was reminded of what the old woman had said to him in their voyage to Buenos Ayres, and of her wager that there was not a person on board the ship but had met with very great misfortunes. He dreamed of Pangloss at every adventure told to him.

"This Pangloss," said he, "would be puzzled to demonstrate his system. I wish that he were here. Certainly, if all things are good, it is in El Dorado and not in the rest of the world."

At length he made choice of a poor man of letters, who had worked ten years for the booksellers of Amsterdam. He judged that there was not in the whole world a trade which could disgust one more.

This philosopher was an honest man; but he had been robbed by his wife, beaten by his son, and abandoned by his daughter who got a Portuguese to run away with her. He had just been deprived of a small employment, on which he subsisted; and he was persecuted by the preachers of Surinam, who took him for a Socinian. We must allow that the others were at least as wretched as he; but Candide hoped that the philosopher would entertain him during the voyage. All the other candidates complained that Candide had done them great injustice; but he appeased them by giving one hundred piastres to each.

WHAT HAPPENED AT SEA TO CANDIDE AND MARTIN

The old philosopher, whose name was Martin, embarked then with Candide for Bordeaux. They had both seen and suffered a great deal; and if the vessel had sailed from Surinam to Japan, by the Cape of Good Hope, the subject of moral and natural evil would have enabled them to entertain one another during the whole voyage.

Candide, however, had one great advantage over Martin, in that he always hoped to see Miss Cunegonde; whereas Martin had nothing at all to hope. Besides, Candide was possessed of money and jewels, and though he had lost one hundred large red sheep, laden with the greatest treasure upon earth; though the knavery of the Dutch skipper still sat heavy upon his mind; yet when he reflected upon what he had still left, and when he mentioned the name of Cunegonde, especially towards the latter end of a repast, he inclined to Pangloss's doctrine.

"But you, Mr. Martin," said he to the philosopher, "what do you think of all this? what are your ideas on moral and natural evil?"

"Sir," answered Martin, "our priests accused me of being a Socinian, but the real fact is I am a Manichean."

"You jest," said Candide; "there are no longer Manicheans in the world."

"I am one," said Martin. "I cannot help it; I know not how to think otherwise."

"Surely you must be possessed by the devil," said Candide.

"He is so deeply concerned in the affairs of this world," answered Martin, "that he may very well be in me, as well as in everybody else; but I own to you that when I cast an eye on this globe, or rather on this little ball, I cannot help thinking that God has abandoned it to some malignant being. I except, always, El Dorado. I scarcely ever knew a city that did not desire the destruction of a neighbouring city, nor a family that did not wish to exterminate some other family. Everywhere the weak execrate the powerful, before whom they cringe; and the powerful beat them like sheep whose wool and flesh they sell. A million regimented assassins, from one extremity of Europe to the other, get their bread by disciplined depredation and murder, for want of more honest employment. Even in those cities which seem to enjoy peace, and where the arts flourish, the inhabitants are devoured by more envy, care, and uneasiness than are experienced by a besieged town. Secret griefs are more cruel than public calamities. In a word I have seen so much, and experienced so much that I am a Manichean."

"There are, however, some things good," said Candide.

"That may be," said Martin; "but I know them not."

In the middle of this dispute they heard the report of cannon; it redoubled every instant. Each took out his glass. They saw two ships in close fight about three miles off. The wind brought both so near to the French vessel that our travellers had the pleasure of seeing the fight at their ease. At length one let off a broadside, so low and so truly aimed, that the other sank to the bottom. Candide and Martin could plainly perceive a hundred men on the deck of the sinking vessel; they raised their hands to heaven and uttered terrible outcries, and the next moment were swallowed up by the sea.

"Well," said Martin, "this is how men treat one another."

"It is true," said Candide; "there is something diabolical in this affair."

While speaking, he saw he knew not what, of a shining red, swimming close to the vessel. They put out the long-boat to see what it could be: it was one of his sheep! Candide was more rejoiced at the recovery of this one sheep than he had been grieved at the loss of the hundred laden with the large diamonds of El Dorado.

The French captain soon saw that the captain of the victorious vessel was a Spaniard, and that the other was a Dutch pirate, and the very same one who had robbed Candide. The immense plunder which this villain had amassed, was buried with him in the sea, and out of the whole only one sheep was saved.

"You see," said Candide to Martin, "that crime is sometimes punished. This rogue of a Dutch skipper has met with the fate he deserved."

"Yes," said Martin; "but why should the passengers be doomed also to destruction? God has punished the knave, and the devil has drowned the rest."

The French and Spanish ships continued their course, and Candide continued his conversation with Martin. They disputed fifteen successive days, and on the last of those fifteen days, they were as far advanced as on the first. But, however, they chatted, they communicated ideas, they consoled each other. Candide caressed his sheep.

"Since I have found thee again," said he, "I may likewise chance to find my Cunegonde."

CANDIDE AND MARTIN, REASONING, DRAW NEAR THE COAST OF FRANCE

At length they descried the coast of France.

"Were you ever in France, Mr. Martin?" said Candide.

"Yes," said Martin, "I have been in several provinces. In some one-half of the people are fools, in others they are too cunning; in some they are weak and simple, in others they affect to be witty; in all, the principal occupation is love, the next is slander, and the third is talking nonsense."

"But, Mr. Martin, have you seen Paris?"

"Yes, I have. All these kinds are found there. It is a chaos—a confused multitude, where everybody seeks pleasure and scarcely any one finds it, at least as it appeared to me. I made a short stay there. On my arrival I was robbed of all I had by pickpockets at the fair of St. Germain. I myself was taken for a robber and was imprisoned for eight days, after which I served as corrector of the press to gain the money necessary for my return to Holland on foot. I knew the whole scribbling rabble, the party rabble, the fanatic rabble. It is said that there are very polite people in that city, and I wish to believe it."

"For my part, I have no curiosity to see France," said Candide. "You may easily imagine that after spending a month at El Dorado I can desire to behold nothing upon earth but Miss Cunegonde. I go to await her at Venice. We shall pass through France on our way to Italy. Will you bear me company?"

"With all my heart," said Martin. "It is said that Venice is fit only for its own nobility, but that strangers meet with a very good reception if they have a good deal of money. I have none of it; you have, therefore I will follow you all over the world."

"But do you believe," said Candide, "that the earth was originally a sea, as we find it asserted in that large book belonging to the captain?"

"I do not believe a word of it," said Martin, "any more than I do of the many ravings which have been published lately."

"But for what end, then, has this world been formed?" said Candide.

"To plague us to death," answered Martin.

"Are you not greatly surprised," continued Candide, "at the love which these two girls of the Oreillons had for those monkeys, of which I have already told you?"

"Not at all," said Martin. "I do not see that that passion was strange. I have seen so many extraordinary things that I have ceased to be surprised."

"Do you believe," said Candide, "that men have always massacred each other as they do to-day, that they have always been liars, cheats, traitors, ingrates, brigands, idiots, thieves, scoundrels, gluttons, drunkards, misers, envious, ambitious, bloody-minded, calumniators, debauchees, fanatics, hypocrites, and fools?"

"Do you believe," said Martin, "that hawks have always eaten pigeons when they have found them?"

"Yes, without doubt," said Candide.

"Well, then," said Martin, "if hawks have always had the same character why should you imagine that men may have changed theirs?"

"Oh!" said Candide, "there is a vast deal of difference, for free will——"

And reasoning thus they arrived at Bordeaux.

WHAT HAPPENED IN FRANCE
TO CANDIDE AND MARTIN

Candide stayed in Bordeaux no longer than was necessary for the selling of a few of the pebbles of El Dorado, and for hiring a good chaise to hold two passengers; for he could not travel without his Philosopher Martin. He was only vexed at parting with his sheep, which he left to the Bordeaux Academy of Sciences, who set as a subject for that year's prize, "to find why this sheep's wool was red;" and the prize was awarded to a learned man of the North, who demonstrated by A plus B minus C divided by Z, that the sheep must be red, and die of the rot.

Meanwhile, all the travellers whom Candide met in the inns along his route, said to him, "We go to Paris." This general eagerness at length gave him, too, a desire to see this capital; and it was not so very great a détour from the road to Venice.

He entered Paris by the suburb of St. Marceau, and fancied that he was in the dirtiest village of Westphalia.

Scarcely was Candide arrived at his inn, than he found himself attacked by a slight illness, caused by fatigue. As he had a very large diamond on his finger, and the people of the inn had taken notice of a prodigiously heavy box among his baggage, there were two physicians to attend him, though he had never sent for them, and two devotees who warmed his broths.

"I remember," Martin said, "also to have been sick at Paris in my first voyage; I was very poor, thus I had neither friends, devotees, nor doctors, and I recovered."

However, what with physic and bleeding, Candide's illness became serious. A parson of the neighborhood came with great meekness to ask for a bill for the other world payable to the bearer. Candide would do nothing for him; but the devotees assured him it was the new fashion. He answered that he was not a man of fashion. Martin wished to throw the priest out of the window. The priest swore that they would not bury Candide. Martin swore that he would bury the priest if he continued to be troublesome. The quarrel grew heated. Martin took him by the shoulders and roughly turned him out of doors; which occasioned great scandal and a law-suit.

Candide got well again, and during his convalescence he had very good company to sup with him. They played high. Candide wondered why it was that the ace never came to him; but Martin was not at all astonished.

Among those who did him the honours of the town was a little Abbé of Perigord, one of those busybodies who are ever alert, officious, forward, fawning, and complaisant; who watch for strangers in their passage through the capital, tell them the scandalous history of the town, and offer them pleasure at all prices. He first took Candide and Martin to La Comédie, where they played a new tragedy. Candide happened to be seated near some of the fashionable wits. This did not prevent his shedding tears at the well-acted scenes. One of these critics at his side said to him between the acts:

"Your tears are misplaced; that is a shocking actress; the

actor who plays with her is yet worse; and the play is still worse than the actors. The author does not know a word of Arabic, yet the scene is in Arabia; moreover he is a man that does not believe in innate ideas; and I will bring you, to-morrow, twenty pamphlets written against him."

"How many dramas have you in France, sir?" said Candide to the Abbé.

"Five or six thousand."

"What a number!" said Candide. "How many good?"

"Fifteen or sixteen," replied the other.

"What a number!" said Martin.

Candide was very pleased with an actress who played Queen Elizabeth in a somewhat insipid tragedy sometimes acted.

"That actress," said he to Martin, "pleases me much; she has a likeness to Miss Cunegonde; I should be very glad to wait upon her."

The Perigordian Abbé offered to introduce him. Candide, brought up in Germany, asked what was the etiquette, and how they treated queens of England in France.

"It is necessary to make distinctions," said the Abbé. "In the provinces one takes them to the inn; in Paris, one respects them when they are beautiful, and throws them on the highway when they are dead."

"Queens on the highway!" said Candide.

"Yes, truly," said Martin, "the Abbé is right. I was in Paris when Miss Monime passed, as the saying is, from this life to the other. She was refused what people call the honours of sepulture—that is to say, of rotting with all the beggars of the neighbourhood in an ugly cemetery; she was interred all alone by her company at the corner of the Rue de Bourgogne, which ought to trouble her much, for she thought nobly."

"That was very uncivil," said Candide.

"What would you have?" said Martin; "these people are made thus. Imagine all contradictions, all possible incompatibilities—you will find them in the government, in the law-courts, in the churches, in the public shows of this droll nation."

"Is it true that they always laugh in Paris?" said Candide.

"Yes," said the Abbé, "but it means nothing, for they complain of everything with great fits of laughter; they even do the most detestable things while laughing."

"Who," said Candide, "is that great pig who spoke so ill of the piece at which I wept, and of the actors who gave me so much pleasure?"

"He is a bad character," answered the Abbé, "who gains his livelihood by saying evil of all plays and of all books. He hates whatever succeeds, as the eunuchs hate those who enjoy; he is one of the serpents of literature who nourish themselves on dirt and spite; he is a folliculaire."

"What is a folliculaire?" said Candide.

"It is," said the Abbé, "a pamphleteer—a Fréron."

Thus Candide, Martin, and the Perigordian conversed on the staircase, while watching every one go out after the performance.

"Although I am eager to see Cunegonde again," said Candide, "I should like to sup with Miss Clairon, for she appears to me admirable."

The Abbé was not the man to approach Miss Clairon, who saw only good company.

"She is engaged for this evening," he said, "but I shall have the honour to take you to the house of a lady of quality, and there you will know Paris as if you had lived in it for years."

Candide, who was naturally curious, let himself be taken to this lady's house, at the end of the Faubourg St. Honoré. The company was occupied in playing faro; a dozen melancholy punters held each in his hand a little pack of cards; a bad record of his misfortunes. Profound silence reigned; pallor was on the faces of the punters, anxiety on that of the banker, and the hostess, sitting near the unpitying banker, noticed with lynx-eyes all the doubled and other increased stakes, as each player dog-eared his cards; she made them turn down the edges again with severe, but polite attention; she showed no vexation for fear of losing her customers. The lady insisted upon being called the Marchioness of Parolignac. Her daughter, aged fifteen, was among the punters, and notified with a covert glance the cheatings of the poor people who tried to repair the cruelties of fate. The Perigordian Abbé, Candide and Martin entered; no one rose, no one saluted them, no one looked at them; all were profoundly occupied with their cards.

"The Baroness of Thunder-ten-Tronckh was more polite," said Candide.

However, the Abbé whispered to the Marchioness, who half rose, honoured Candide with a gracious smile, and Martin with a condescending nod; she gave a seat and a pack of cards to Candide, who lost fifty thousand francs in two deals, after which they supped very gaily, and everyone was astonished that Candide was not moved by his loss.

The servants said among themselves, in the language of servants, "Some English lord is here this evening."

The supper passed at first like most Parisian suppers, in silence, followed by a noise of words which could not be distinguished, then with pleasantries of which most were insipid, with false news, with bad reasoning, a little politics, and much evil speaking; they also discussed new books.

"Have you seen," said the Perigordian Abbé, "the romance of Sieur Gauchat, Doctor of Divinity?"

"Yes," answered one of the guests, "but I have not been able to finish it. We have a crowd of silly writings, but all together do not approach the impertinence of 'Gauchat, Doctor of Divinity'. I am so satiated with the great number of detestable books with which we are inundated that I am reduced to punting at faro."

"And the Mélanges of Archdeacon Trublet, what do you say of that?" said the Abbé.

"Ah!" said the Marchioness of Parolignac, "The wearisome mortal! How curiously he repeats to you all that the world knows! How heavily he discusses that which is not worth the trouble of lightly remarking upon! How, without wit, he appropriates the wit of others! How he spoils what he steals! How he disgusts me! But he will disgust me no longer—it is enough to have read a few of the Archdeacon's pages."

There was at table a wise man of taste, who supported the Marchioness. They spoke afterwards of tragedies; the lady asked why there were tragedies which were sometimes played and which could not be read. The man of taste explained very well how a piece could have some interest, and have almost no merit; he proved in few words that it was not enough to introduce one or two of those situations which one finds in all romances, and which always seduce the spectator, but that it was necessary to be new without being odd, often sublime and always natural, to know the human heart and to make it speak; to be a great poet without allowing any person in the piece to appear to be a poet; to know language perfectly—to speak it with purity, with continuous harmony and without rhythm ever taking anything from sense.

"Whoever," added he, "does not observe all these rules can produce one or two tragedies, applauded at a theatre, but he will never be counted in the ranks of good writers. There are very few good tragedies; some are idylls in dialogue, well written and well rhymed, others political reasonings which lull to sleep, or amplifications which repel; others demoniac dreams in barbarous style, interrupted in sequence, with long apostrophes to the gods, because they do not know how to speak to men, with false maxims, with bombastic commonplaces!"

Candide listened with attention to this discourse, and conceived a great idea of the speaker, and as the Marchioness had taken care to place him beside her, he leaned towards her and took the liberty of asking who was the man who had spoken so well.

"He is a scholar," said the lady, "who does not play, whom the Abbé sometimes brings to supper; he is perfectly at home among tragedies and books, and he has written a tragedy which was hissed, and a book of which nothing has ever been seen outside his bookseller's shop excepting the copy which he dedicated to me."

"The great man!" said Candide. "He is another Pangloss!"

Then, turning towards him, he said:

"Sir, you think doubtless that all is for the best in the moral and physical world, and that nothing could be otherwise than it is?"

"I, sir!" answered the scholar, "I know nothing of all that; I find that all goes awry with me; that no one knows either what is his rank, nor what is his condition, what he does nor what he ought to do; and that except supper, which is always gay, and where there appears to be enough concord, all the rest of the time is passed in impertinent quarrels; Jansenist against Molinist, Parliament against the Church, men of letters against men of letters, courtesans against courtesans, financiers against the people, wives against husbands, relatives against relatives—it is eternal war."

"I have seen the worst," Candide replied. "But a wise man, who since has had the misfortune to be hanged, taught me that all is marvellously well; these are but the shadows on a beautiful picture."

"Your hanged man mocked the world," said Martin. "The shadows are horrible blots."

"They are men who make the blots," said Candide, "and they cannot be dispensed with."

"It is not their fault then," said Martin.

Most of the punters, who understood nothing of this language, drank, and Martin reasoned with the scholar, and Candide related some of his adventures to his hostess.

After supper the Marchioness took Candide into her boudoir, and made him sit upon a sofa.

"Ah, well!" said she to him, "you love desperately Miss Cunegonde of Thunder-ten-Tronckh?"

"Yes, madame," answered Candide.

The Marchioness replied to him with a tender smile:

"You answer me like a young man from Westphalia. A Frenchman would have said, 'It is true that I have loved Miss Cunegonde, but seeing you, madame, I think I no longer love her.'"

"Alas! madame," said Candide, "I will answer you as you wish."

"Your passion for her," said the Marchioness, "commenced by picking up her handkerchief. I wish that you would pick up my garter."

"With all my heart," said Candide. And he picked it up.

"But I wish that you would put it on," said the lady.

And Candide put it on.

"You see," said she, "you are a foreigner. I sometimes make my Parisian lovers languish for fifteen days, but I give myself to you the first night because one must do the honours of one's country to a young man from Westphalia."

The lady having perceived two enormous diamonds upon the hands of the young foreigner praised them with such good faith that from Candide's fingers they passed to her own.

Candide, returning with the Perigordian Abbé, felt some remorse in having been unfaithful to Miss Cunegonde. The Abbé sympathised in his trouble; he had had but a light part of the fifty thousand francs lost at play and of the value of the two brilliants, half given, half extorted. His design was to profit as much as he could by the advantages which the acquaintance of Candide could procure for him. He spoke much of Cunegonde, and Candide told him that he should ask forgiveness of that beautiful one for his infidelity when he should see her in Venice.

The Abbé redoubled his politeness and attentions, and took a tender interest in all that Candide said, in all that he did, in all that he wished to do.

"And so, sir, you have a rendezvous at Venice?"

"Yes, monsieur Abbé," answered Candide. "It is absolutely necessary that I go to meet Miss Cunegonde."

And then the pleasure of talking of that which he loved induced him to relate, according to his custom, part of his adventures with the fair Westphalian.

"I believe," said the Abbé, "that Miss Cunegonde has a great deal of wit, and that she writes charming letters?"

"I have never received any from her," said Candide, "for being expelled from the castle on her account I had not an opportunity for writing to her. Soon after that I heard she was dead; then I found her alive; then I lost her again; and last of all, I sent an express to her two thousand five hundred leagues from here, and I wait for an answer."

The Abbé listened attentively, and seemed to be in a brown study. He soon took his leave of the two foreigners after a most tender embrace.

The following day Candide received, on awaking, a letter couched in these terms:

"My very dear love, for eight days I have been ill in this

town. I learn that you are here. I would fly to your arms if I could but move. I was informed of your passage at Bordeaux, where I left faithful Cacambo and the old woman, who are to follow me very soon. The Governor of Buenos Ayres has taken all, but there remains to me your heart. Come! Your presence will either give me life or kill me with pleasure."

This charming, this unhoped-for letter transported Candide with an inexpressible joy, and the illness of his dear Cunegonde overwhelmed him with grief. Divided between those two passions, he took his gold and his diamonds and hurried away, with Martin, to the hotel where Miss Cunegonde was lodged. He entered her room trembling, his heart palpitating, his voice sobbing; he wished to open the curtains of the bed, and asked for a light.

"Take care what you do," said the servant-maid; "the light hurts her," and immediately she drew the curtain again.

"My dear Cunegonde," said Candide, weeping, "how are you? If you cannot see me, at least speak to me."

"She cannot speak," said the maid.

The lady then put a plump hand out from the bed, and Candide bathed it with his tears and afterwards filled it with diamonds, leaving a bag of gold upon the easy chair.

In the midst of these transports in came an officer, followed by the Abbé and a file of soldiers.

"There," said he, "are the two suspected foreigners," and at the same time he ordered them to be seized and carried to prison.

"Travellers are not treated thus in El Dorado," said Candide.

"I am more a Manichean now than ever," said Martin.

"But pray, sir, where are you going to carry us?" said Candide.

"To a dungeon," answered the officer.

Martin, having recovered himself a little, judged that the lady who acted the part of Cunegonde was a cheat, that the Perigordian Abbé was a knave who had imposed upon the honest simplicity of Candide, and that the officer was another knave whom they might easily silence.

Candide, advised by Martin and impatient to see the real Cunegonde, rather than expose himself before a court of justice, proposed to the officer to give him three small diamonds, each worth about three thousand pistoles.

"Ah, sir," said the man with the ivory baton, "had you committed all the imaginable crimes you would be to me the most honest man in the world. Three diamonds! Each worth three thousand pistoles! Sir, instead of carrying you to jail I would lose my life to serve you. There are orders for arresting all foreigners, but leave it to me. I have a brother at Dieppe in Normandy! I'll conduct you thither, and if you have a diamond to give him he'll take as much care of you as I would."

"And why," said Candide, "should all foreigners be arrested?"

"It is," the Perigordian Abbé then made answer, "because a poor beggar of the country of Atrébatie heard some foolish things said. This induced him to commit a parricide, not such as that of 1610 in the month of May, but such as that of 1594 in the month of December, and such as others which have been committed in other years and other months by other poor devils who had heard nonsense spoken."

The officer then explained what the Abbé meant.

"Ah, the monsters!" cried Candide. "What horrors among a people who dance and sing! Is there no way of getting quickly out of this country where monkeys provoke tigers? I have seen no bears in my country, but men I have beheld nowhere except in El Dorado. In the name of God, sir, conduct me to Venice, where I am to await Miss Cunegonde."

"I can conduct you no further than lower Normandy," said the officer.

Immediately he ordered his irons to be struck off, acknowledged himself mistaken, sent away his men, set out with Candide and Martin for Dieppe, and left them in the care of his brother.

There was then a small Dutch ship in the harbour. The Norman, who by the virtue of three more diamonds had become the most subservient of men, put Candide and his attendants on board a vessel that was just ready to set sail for Portsmouth in England.

This was not the way to Venice, but Candide thought he had made his way out of hell, and reckoned that he would soon have an opportunity for resuming his journey.

CANDIDE AND MARTIN TOUCHED UPON THE COAST OF ENGLAND, AND WHAT THEY SAW THERE

"Ah, Pangloss! Pangloss! Ah, Martin! Martin! Ah, my dear Cunegonde, what sort of a world is this?" said Candide on board the Dutch ship.

"Something very foolish and abominable," said Martin.

"You know England? Are they as foolish there as in France?"

"It is another kind of folly," said Martin. "You know that these two nations are at war for a few acres of snow in Canada, and that they spend over this beautiful war much more than Canada is worth. To tell you exactly, whether there are more people fit to send to a madhouse in one country than the other, is what my imperfect intelligence will not permit. I only know in general that the people we are going to see are very atrabilious."

Talking thus they arrived at Portsmouth. The coast was lined with crowds of people, whose eyes were fixed on a fine man kneeling, with his eyes bandaged, on board one of the men of war in the harbour. Four soldiers stood opposite to this man; each of them fired three balls at his head, with all the calmness in the world; and the whole assembly went away very well satisfied.

"What is all this?" said Candide; "And what demon is it that exercises his empire in this country?"

He then asked who was that fine man who had been killed with so much ceremony. They answered, he was an Admiral.

"And why kill this Admiral?"

"It is because he did not kill a sufficient number of men himself. He gave battle to a French Admiral; and it has been proved that he was not near enough to him."

"But," replied Candide, "the French Admiral was as far from the English Admiral."

"There is no doubt of it; but in this country it is found good, from time to time, to kill one Admiral to encourage the others."

Candide was so shocked and bewildered by what he saw and heard, that he would not set foot on shore, and he made a bargain with the Dutch skipper (were he even to rob him like the Surinam captain) to conduct him without delay to Venice.

The skipper was ready in two days. They coasted France; they passed in sight of Lisbon, and Candide trembled. They passed through the Straits, and entered the Mediterranean. At last they landed at Venice.

"God be praised!" said Candide, embracing Martin. "It is here that I shall see again my beautiful Cunegonde. I trust Cacambo as myself. All is well, all will be well, all goes as well as possible."

OF PAQUETTE AND FRIAR GIROFLÉE

Upon their arrival at Venice, Candide went to search for Cacambo at every inn and coffee-house, and among all the ladies of pleasure, but to no purpose. He sent every day to inquire on all the ships that came in. But there was no news of Cacambo.

"What!" said he to Martin, "I have had time to voyage from Surinam to Bordeaux, to go from Bordeaux to Paris, from Paris to Dieppe, from Dieppe to Portsmouth, to coast along Portugal and Spain, to cross the whole Mediterranean, to spend some months, and yet the beautiful Cunegonde has not arrived! Instead of her I have only met a Parisian wench and a Perigordian Abbé. Cunegonde is dead without doubt, and there is nothing for me but to die. Alas! how much better it would have been for me to have remained in the paradise of El Dorado than to come back to this cursed Europe! You are in the right, my dear Martin: all is misery and illusion."

He fell into a deep melancholy, and neither went to see the opera, nor any of the other diversions of the Carnival; nay, he was proof against the temptations of all the ladies.

"You are in truth very simple," said Martin to him, "if you imagine that a mongrel valet, who has five or six millions in his pocket, will go to the other end of the world to seek your mistress and bring her to you to Venice. If he finds her, he will keep her to himself; if he does not find her, he will get another. I advise you to forget your valet Cacambo and your mistress Cunegonde."

Martin was not consoling. Candide's melancholy increased; and Martin continued to prove to him that there was very little virtue or happiness upon earth, except perhaps in El Dorado, where nobody could gain admittance.

While they were disputing on this important subject and waiting for Cunegonde, Candide saw a young Theatin friar in St. Mark's Piazza, holding a girl on his arm. The Theatin looked fresh coloured, plump, and vigorous; his eyes were sparkling, his air assured, his look lofty, and his step bold. The girl was very pretty, and sang; she looked amorously at her Theatin, and from time to time pinched his fat cheeks.

"At least you will allow me," said Candide to Martin, "that these two are happy. Hitherto I have met with none but unfortunate people in the whole habitable globe, except in El Dorado; but as to this pair, I would venture to lay a wager that they are very happy."

"I lay you they are not," said Martin.

"We need only ask them to dine with us," said Candide, "and you will see whether I am mistaken."

Immediately he accosted them, presented his compliments, and invited them to his inn to eat some macaroni, with Lombard partridges, and caviare, and to drink some Montepulciano, Lachrymæ Christi, Cyprus and Samos wine. The girl blushed, the Theatin accepted the invitation and she followed him, casting her eyes on Candide with confusion and surprise, and dropping a few tears. No sooner had she set foot in Candide's apartment than she cried out:

"Ah! Mr. Candide does not know Paquette again."

Candide had not viewed her as yet with attention, his thoughts being entirely taken up with Cunegonde; but recollecting her as she spoke.

"Alas!" said he, "My poor child, it is you who reduced Doctor Pangloss to the beautiful condition in which I saw him?"

"Alas! it was I, sir, indeed," answered Paquette. "I see that you have heard all. I have been informed of the frightful disasters that befell the family of my lady Baroness, and the fair Cunegonde. I swear to you that my fate has been scarcely less sad. I was very innocent when you knew me. A Grey Friar, who was my confessor, easily seduced me. The consequences were terrible. I was obliged to quit the castle some time after the Baron had sent you away with kicks on the backside. If a famous surgeon had not taken compassion on me, I should have died. For some time I was this surgeon's mistress, merely out of gratitude. His wife, who was mad with jealousy, beat me every day unmercifully; she was a fury. The surgeon was one of the ugliest of men, and I the most wretched of women, to be continually beaten for a man I did not love. You know, sir, what a dangerous thing it is for an ill-natured woman to be married to a doctor. Incensed at the behaviour of his wife, he one day gave her so effectual a remedy to cure her of a slight cold, that she died two hours after, in most horrid convulsions. The wife's relations prosecuted the husband; he took flight, and I was thrown into jail. My innocence would not have saved me if I had not been good-looking. The judge set me free, on condition that he succeeded the surgeon. I was soon supplanted by a rival, turned out of doors quite destitute, and obliged to continue this abominable trade, which appears so pleasant to you men, while to us women it is the utmost abyss of misery. I have come to exercise the profession at Venice. Ah! Sir, if you could only imagine what it is to be obliged to caress indifferently an old merchant, a lawyer, a monk, a gondolier, an abbé, to be exposed to abuse and insults; to be often reduced to borrowing a petticoat, only to go and have it raised by a disagreeable man; to be robbed by one of what one has earned from another; to be subject to the extortions of the officers of justice; and to have in prospect only a frightful old age, a hospital, and a dung-hill; you would conclude that I am one of the most unhappy creatures in the world."

Paquette thus opened her heart to honest Candide, in the presence of Martin, who said to his friend:

"You see that already I have won half the wager."

Friar Giroflée stayed in the dining-room, and drank a glass or two of wine while he was waiting for dinner.

"But," said Candide to Paquette, "you looked so gay and content when I met you; you sang and you behaved so lovingly to the Theatin, that you seemed to me as happy as you pretend to be now the reverse."

"Ah! Sir," answered Paquette, "this is one of the miseries of the trade. Yesterday I was robbed and beaten by an officer; yet to-day I must put on good humour to please a friar."

Candide wanted no more convincing; he owned that Martin was in the right. They sat down to table with Paquette and the Theatin; the repast was entertaining; and towards the end they conversed with all confidence.

"Father," said Candide to the Friar, "you appear to me to enjoy a state that all the world might envy; the flower of health shines in your face, your expression makes plain your happiness; you have a very pretty girl for your recreation, and you seem well satisfied with your state as a Theatin."

"My faith, sir," said Friar Giroflée, "I wish that all the

Theatins were at the bottom of the sea. I have been tempted a hundred times to set fire to the convent, and go and become a Turk. My parents forced me at the age of fifteen to put on this detestable habit, to increase the fortune of a cursed elder brother, whom God confound. Jealousy, discord, and fury, dwell in the convent. It is true I have preached a few bad sermons that have brought me in a little money, of which the prior stole half, while the rest serves to maintain my girls; but when I return at night to the monastery, I am ready to dash my head against the walls of the dormitory; and all my fellows are in the same case."

Martin turned towards Candide with his usual coolness.

"Well," said he, "have I not won the whole wager?"

Candide gave two thousand piastres to Paquette, and one thousand to Friar Giroflée.

"I'll answer for it," said he, "that with this they will be happy."

"I do not believe it at all," said Martin; "you will, perhaps, with these piastres only render them the more unhappy."

"Let that be as it may," said Candide, "but one thing consoles me. I see that we often meet with those whom we expected never to see more; so that, perhaps, as I have found my red sheep and Paquette, it may well be that I shall also find Cunegonde."

"I wish," said Martin, "she may one day make you very happy; but I doubt it very much."

"You are very hard of belief." said Candide.

"I have lived." said Martin.

"You see those gondoliers," said Candide, "are they not perpetually singing?"

"You do not see them," said Martin, "at home with their wives and brats. The Doge has his troubles, the gondoliers have theirs. It is true that, all things considered, the life of a gondolier is preferable to that of a Doge; but I believe the difference to be so trifling that it is not worth the trouble of examining."

"People talk," said Candide, "of the Senator Pococurante, who lives in that fine palace on the Brenta, where he entertains foreigners in the politest manner. They pretend that this man has never felt any uneasiness."

"I should be glad to see such a rarity." said Martin.

Candide immediately sent to ask the Lord Pococurante permission to wait upon him the next day.

THE VISIT TO LORD POCOCURANTE, A NOBLE VENETIAN

Candide and Martin went in a gondola on the Brenta, and arrived at the palace of the noble Signor Pococurante. The gardens, laid out with taste, were adorned with fine marble statues. The palace was beautifully built. The master of the house was a man of sixty, and very rich. He received the two travellers with polite indifference, which put Candide a little out of countenance, but was not at all disagreeable to Martin.

First, two pretty girls, very neatly dressed, served them with chocolate, which was frothed exceedingly well. Candide could not refrain from commending their beauty, grace, and address.

"They are good enough creatures," said the Senator, "I make them lie with me sometimes, for I am very tired of the ladies of the town, of their coquetries, of their jealousies, of their quarrels, of their humours, of their pettinesses, of their prides, of their follies, and of the sonnets which one must make, or have made, for them. But after all, these two girls begin to weary me."

After breakfast, Candide walking into a long gallery was surprised by the beautiful pictures. He asked, by what master were the two first.

"They are by Raphael," said the Senator. "I bought them at a great price, out of vanity, some years ago. They are said to be the finest things in Italy, but they do not please me at all. The colours are too dark, the figures are not sufficiently rounded, nor in good relief; the draperies in no way resemble stuffs. In a word, whatever may be said, I do not find there a true imitation of nature. I only care for a picture when I think I see nature itself; and there are none of this sort. I have a great many pictures, but I prize them very little."

While they were waiting for dinner Pococurante ordered a concert. Candide found the music delicious.

"This noise," said the Senator, "may amuse one for half an hour; but if it were to last longer it would grow tiresome to everybody, though they durst not own it. Music today is only the art of executing difficult things, and that which is only difficult cannot please long. Perhaps I should be fonder of the opera if they had not found the secret of making of it a monster which shocks me. Let who will go to see bad tragedies set to music, where the scenes are contrived for no other end than to introduce two or three songs ridiculously out of place, to show off an actress's voice. Let who will, or who can, die away with pleasure at the sight of a eunuch quavering the rôle of Cæsar, or of Cato, and strutting awkwardly upon the stage. For my part I have long since renounced those paltry entertainments which constitute the glory of modern Italy, and are purchased so dearly by sovereigns."

Candide disputed the point a little, but with discretion. Martin was entirely of the Senator's opinion.

They sat down to table, and after an excellent dinner they

went into the library. Candide, seeing a Homer magnificently bound, commended the virtuoso on his good taste.

"There," said he, "is a book that was once the delight of the great Pangloss, the best philosopher in Germany."

"It is not mine." answered Pococurante coolly. "They used at one time to make me believe that I took a pleasure in reading him. But that continual repetition of battles, so extremely like one another; those gods that are always active without doing anything decisive; that Helen who is the cause of the war, and who yet scarcely appears in the piece; that Troy, so long besieged without being taken; all these together caused me great weariness. I have sometimes asked learned men whether they were not as weary as I of that work. Those who were sincere have owned to me that the poem made them fall asleep; yet it was necessary to have it in their library as a monument of antiquity, or like those rusty medals which are no longer of use in commerce."

"But your Excellency does not think thus of Virgil?" said Candide.

"I grant," said the Senator, "that the second, fourth, and sixth books of his Æneid are excellent, but as for his pious Æneas, his strong Cloanthus, his friend Achates, his little Ascanius, his silly King Latinus, his bourgeois Amata, his insipid Lavinia, I think there can be nothing more flat and disagreeable. I prefer Tasso a good deal, or even the soporific tales of Ariosto."

"May I presume to ask you, sir," said Candide, "whether you do not receive a great deal of pleasure from reading Horace?"

"There are maxims in this writer," answered Pococurante, "from which a man of the world may reap great benefit, and being written in energetic verse they are more easily impressed upon the memory. But I care little for his journey to Brundusium, and his account of a bad dinner, or of his low quarrel between one Rupilius whose words he says were full of poisonous filth, and another whose language was imbued with vinegar. I have read with much distaste his indelicate verses against old women and witches; nor do I see any merit in telling his friend Mæcenas that if he will but rank him in the choir of lyric poets, his lofty head shall touch the stars. Fools admire everything in an author of reputation. For my part, I read only to please myself. I like only that which serves my purpose."

Candide, having been educated never to judge for himself, was much surprised at what he heard. Martin found there was a good deal of reason in Pococurante's remarks.

"Oh! Here is Cicero," said Candide. "Here is the great man whom I fancy you are never tired of reading."

"I never read him," replied the Venetian. "What is it to me whether he pleads for Rabirius or Cluentius? I try causes enough myself; his philosophical works seem to me better, but when I found that he doubted of everything, I concluded that I knew as much as he, and that I had no need of a guide to learn ignorance."

"Ha! Here are four-score volumes of the Academy of Sciences," cried Martin. "Perhaps there is something valuable in this collection."

"There might be," said Pococurante, "if only one of those rakers of rubbish had shown how to make pins; but in all these volumes there is nothing but chimerical systems, and not a single useful thing."

"And what dramatic works I see here," said Candide, "in Italian, Spanish, and French."

"Yes," replied the Senator, "there are three thousand, and not three dozen of them good for anything. As to those collections of sermons, which altogether are not worth a single page of Seneca, and those huge volumes of theology, you may well imagine that neither I nor anyone else ever opens them."

Martin saw some shelves filled with English books.

"I have a notion," said he, "that a Republican must be greatly pleased with most of these books, which are written with a spirit of freedom."

"Yes," answered Pococurante, "it is noble to write as one thinks; this is the privilege of humanity. In all our Italy we write only what we do not think; those who inhabit the country of the Cæsars and the Antoninuses dare not acquire a single idea without the permission of a Dominican friar. I should be pleased with the liberty which inspires the English genius if passion and party spirit did not corrupt all that is estimable in this precious liberty."

Candide, observing a Milton, asked whether he did not look upon this author as a great man.

"Who?" said Pococurante, "That barbarian, who writes a long commentary in ten books of harsh verse on the first chapter of Genesis; that coarse imitator of the Greeks, who disfigures the Creation, and who, while Moses represents the Eternal producing the world by a word, makes the Messiah take a great pair of compasses from the armoury of heaven to circumscribe His work? How can I have any esteem for a writer who has spoiled Tasso's hell and the devil, who transforms Lucifer sometimes into a toad and other times into a pigmy, who makes him repeat the same things a hundred times, who makes him dispute on theology, who, by a serious imitation of Ariosto's comic invention of firearms, represents the devils cannonading in heaven? Neither I nor any man in Italy could take pleasure in those melancholy extravagances; and the marriage of Sin and Death, and the snakes brought forth by Sin, are enough to turn the stomach of any one with the least taste;

and his long description of a pest-house is good only for a grave-digger. This obscure, whimsical, and disagreeable poem was despised upon its first publication, and I only treat it now as it was treated in its own country by contemporaries. For the matter of that I say what I think, and I care very little whether others think as I do."

Candide was grieved at this speech, for he had a respect for Homer and was fond of Milton.

"Alas!" said he softly to Martin, "I am afraid that this man holds our German poets in very great contempt."

"There would not be much harm in that," said Martin.

"Oh! What a superior man," said Candide below his breath. "What a great genius is this Pococurante! Nothing can please him."

After their survey of the library they went down into the garden, where Candide praised its several beauties.

"I know of nothing in so bad a taste," said the master. "All you see here is merely trifling. After tomorrow I will have it planted with a nobler design."

"Well," said Candide to Martin when they had taken their leave, "you will agree that this is the happiest of mortals, for he is above everything he possesses."

"But do you not see," answered Martin, "that he is disgusted with all he possesses? Plato observed a long while ago that those stomachs are not the best that reject all sorts of food."

"But is there not a pleasure," said Candide, "in criticising everything, in pointing out faults where others see nothing but beauties?"

"That is to say," replied Martin, "that there is some pleasure in having no pleasure."

"Well, well," said Candide, "I find that I shall be the only happy man when I am blessed with the sight of my dear Cunegonde."

"It is always well to hope," said Martin.

However, the days and the weeks passed. Cacambo did not come, and Candide was so overwhelmed with grief that he did not even reflect that Paquette and Friar Giroflée did not return to thank him.

OF A SUPPER WHICH
CANDIDE AND MARTIN
TOOK WITH SIX STRANGERS,
AND WHO THEY WERE

One evening that Candide and Martin were going to sit down to supper with some foreigners who lodged in the same inn, a man whose complexion was as black as soot, came behind Candide, and taking him by the arm, said:

"Get yourself ready to go along with us; do not fail."

Upon this he turned round and saw—Cacambo! Nothing but the sight of Cunegonde could have astonished and delighted him more. He was on the point of going mad with joy. He embraced his dear friend.

"Cunegonde is here, without doubt; where is she? Take me to her that I may die of joy in her company."

"Cunegonde is not here," said Cacambo, "she is at Constantinople."

"Oh, heavens! At Constantinople! But were she in China I would fly thither; let us be off."

"We shall set out after supper," replied Cacambo. "I can tell you nothing more; I am slave, my master awaits me, I must serve him at table; speak not a word, eat, and then get ready."

Candide, distracted between joy and grief, delighted at seeing his faithful agent again, astonished at finding him a slave, filled with the fresh hope of recovering his mistress, his heart palpitating, his understanding confused, sat down to table with Martin, who saw all these scenes quite unconcerned, and with six strangers who had come to spend the Carnival at Venice.

Cacambo waited at table upon one of the strangers; towards the end of the entertainment he drew near his master, and whispered in his ear:

"Sire, your Majesty may start when you please, the vessel is ready."

On saying these words he went out. The company in great surprise looked at one another without speaking a word, when another slave approached his master and said to him:

"Sire, your Majesty's chaise is at Padua, and the boat is ready.

The master gave a nod and the servant went away. The company all stared at one another again, and their surprise redoubled. A third valet came up to a third stranger, saying:

"Sire, believe me, your Majesty ought not to stay here any longer. I am going to get everything ready."

And immediately he disappeared. Candide and Martin did not doubt that this was a masquerade of the Carnival. Then a fourth domestic said to a fourth master:

"Your Majesty may depart when you please."

Saying this he went away like the rest. The fifth valet said the same thing to the fifth master. But the sixth valet spoke differently to the sixth stranger, who sat near Candide. He said to him:

"Faith, Sire, they will no longer give credit to your Majesty nor to me, and we may perhaps both of us be put in jail this very night. Therefore I will take care of myself. Adieu."

The slaves and servants being all gone, the six strangers,

with Candide and Martin, remained in a profound silence. At length Candide broke it.

"Gentlemen," said he, "this is a very good joke indeed, but why should you all be kings? For me I own that neither Martin nor I is a king."

Cacambos master then gravely answered in Italian:

"I am not at all joking. My name is Achmet III. I was Grand Sultan many years. I dethroned my brother; my nephew dethroned me, my viziers were beheaded, and I am condemned to end my days in the old Seraglio. My nephew, the great Sultan Mahmoud, permits me to travel sometimes for my health, and I am come to spend the Carnival at Venice."

A young man who sat next to Achmet, spoke then as follows:

"My name is Ivan. I was once Emperor of all the Russias, but was dethroned in my cradle. My parents were confined in prison and I was educated there; yet I am sometimes allowed to travel in company with persons who act as guards; and I am come to spend the Carnival at Venice."

The third said:

"I am Charles Edward, King of England; my father has resigned all his legal rights to me. I have fought in defense of them; and above eight hundred of my adherents have been hanged, drawn, and quartered. I have been confined in prison; I am going to Rome, to pay a visit to the King, my father, who was dethroned as well as myself and my grandfather, and I am come to spend the Carnival at Venice."

The fourth spoke thus in his turn:

"I am the King of Poland; the fortune of war has stripped me of my hereditary dominions; my father underwent the same vicissitudes; I resign myself to Providence in the same manner as Sultan Achmet, the Emperor Ivan, and King Charles

Edward, whom God long preserve; and I am come to the Carnival at Venice."

The fifth said:

"I am King of Poland also; I have been twice dethroned; but Providence has given me another country, where I have done more good than all the Sarmatian kings were ever capable of doing on the banks of the Vistula; I resign myself likewise to Providence, and am come to pass the Carnival at Venice."

It was now the sixth monarch's turn to speak:

"Gentlemen," said he, "I am not so great a prince as any of you; however, I am a king. I am Theodore, elected King of Corsica; I had the title of Majesty, and now I am scarcely treated as a gentleman. I have coined money, and now am not worth a farthing; I have had two secretaries of state, and now I have scarce a valet; I have seen myself on a throne, and I have seen myself upon straw in a common jail in London. I am afraid that I shall meet with the same treatment here though, like your majesties, I am come to see the Carnival at Venice."

The other five kings listened to this speech with generous compassion. Each of them gave twenty sequins to King Theodore to buy him clothes and linen; and Candide made him a present of a diamond worth two thousand sequins.

"Who can this private person be," said the five kings to one another, "who is able to give, and really has given, a hundred times as much as any of us?"

Just as they rose from table, in came four Serene Highnesses, who had also been stripped of their territories by the fortune of war, and were come to spend the Carnival at Venice. But Candide paid no regard to these newcomers, his thoughts were entirely employed on his voyage to Constantinople, in search of his beloved Cunegonde.

CANDIDE'S VOYAGE
TO CONSTANTINOPLE

The faithful Cacambo had already prevailed upon the Turkish skipper, who was to conduct the Sultan Achmet to Constantinople, to receive Candide and Martin on his ship. They both embarked after having made their obeisance to his miserable Highness.

"You see," said Candide to Martin on the way, "we supped with six dethroned kings, and of those six there was one to whom I gave charity. Perhaps there are many other princes yet more unfortunate. For my part, I have only lost a hundred sheep; and now I am flying into Cunegonde's arms. My dear Martin, yet once more Pangloss was right: all is for the best."

"I wish it," answered Martin.

"But," said Candide, "it was a very strange adventure we met with at Venice. It has never before been seen or heard that six dethroned kings have supped together at a public inn."

"It is not more extraordinary," said Martin, "than most of the things that have happened to us. It is a very common thing for kings to be dethroned; and as for the honour we have had of supping in their company, it is a trifle not worth our attention."

No sooner had Candide got on board the vessel than he flew to his old valet and friend Cacambo, and tenderly embraced him.

"Well," said he, "what news of Cunegonde? Is she still a prodigy of beauty? Does she love me still? How is she? Thou hast doubtless bought her a palace at Constantinople?"

"My dear Candide," answered Cacambo, "Cunegonde washes dishes on the banks of the Propontis, in the service of a prince, who has very few dishes to wash; she is a slave in the family of an ancient sovereign named Ragotsky, to whom the Grand Turk allows three crowns a day in his exile. But what is worse still is, that she has lost her beauty and has become horribly ugly."

"Well, handsome or ugly," replied Candide, "I am a man of honour, and it is my duty to love her still. But how came she to be reduced to so abject a state with the five or six millions that you took to her?"

"Ah!" said Cacambo, "was I not to give two million to Senor Don Fernando d'Ibaraa, y Figueora, y Mascarenes, y Lampourdos, y Souza, Governor of Buenos Ayres, for permitting Miss Cunegonde to come away? And did not a corsair bravely rob us of all the rest? Did not this corsair carry us to Cape Matapan, to Milo, to Nicaria, to Samos, to Petra, to the Dardanelles, to Marmora, to Scutari? Cunegonde and the old woman serve the prince I now mentioned to you, and I am slave to the dethroned Sultan."

"What a series of shocking calamities!" cried Candide. "But after all, I have some diamonds left; and I may easily pay Cunegonde's ransom. Yet it is a pity that she is grown so ugly."

Then, turning towards Martin: "Who do you think," said he, "is most to be pitied—the Sultan Achmet, the Emperor Ivan, King Charles Edward, or I?"

"How should I know!" answered Martin. "I must see into their hearts to be able to tell."

"Ah!" said Candide, "If Pangloss were here, he could tell."

"I know not," said Martin, "in what sort of scales your Pangloss would weigh the misfortunes of mankind and set a just estimate on their sorrows. All that I can presume to say is, that there are millions of people upon earth who have a hundred times more to complain of than King Charles Edward, the Emperor Ivan, or the Sultan Achmet."

"That may well be," said Candide.

In a few days they reached the Bosphorus, and Candide began by paying a very high ransom for Cacambo. Then without losing time, he and his companions went on board a galley, in order to search on the banks of the Propontis for his Cunegonde, however ugly she might have become.

Among the crew there were two slaves who rowed very badly, and to whose bare shoulders the Levantine captain would now and then apply blows from a bull's pizzle. Candide, from a natural impulse, looked at these two slaves more attentively than at the other oarsmen, and approached them with pity. Their features though greatly disfigured, had a slight resemblance to those of Pangloss and the unhappy Jesuit and Westphalian Baron, brother to Miss Cunegonde. This moved and saddened him. He looked at them still more attentively.

"Indeed," said he to Cacambo, "if I had not seen Master Pangloss hanged, and if I had not had the misfortune to kill the Baron, I should think it was they that were rowing."

At the names of the Baron and of Pangloss, the two galley-slaves uttered a loud cry, held fast by the seat, and let drop their oars. The captain ran up to them and redoubled his blows with the bull's pizzle.

"Stop! Stop! Sir," cried Candide. "I will give you what money you please."

"What! It is Candide!" said one of the slaves.

"What! It is Candide!" said the other.

"Do I dream?" cried Candide. "Am I awake? Or am I on board a galley? Is this the Baron whom I killed? Is this Master Pangloss whom I saw hanged?"

"It is we! It is we!" answered they.

"Well! Is this the great philosopher?" said Martin.

"Ah! captain," said Candide, "what ransom will you take for Monsieur de Thunder-ten-Tronckh, one of the first barons of the empire, and for Monsieur Pangloss, the profoundest metaphysician in Germany?"

"Dog of a Christian," answered the Levantine captain, "since these two dogs of Christian slaves are barons and metaphysicians, which I doubt not are high dignities in their country, you shall give me fifty thousand sequins."

"You shall have them, sir. Carry me back at once to Constantinople, and you shall receive the money directly. But no; carry me first to Miss Cunegonde."

Upon the first proposal made by Candide, however, the Levantine captain had already tacked about, and made the crew ply their oars quicker than a bird cleaves the air.

Candide embraced the Baron and Pangloss a hundred times.

"And how happened it, my dear Baron, that I did not kill you? And, my dear Pangloss, how came you to life again after being hanged? And why are you both in a Turkish galley?"

"And it is true that my dear sister is in this country?" said the Baron.

"Yes," answered Cacambo.

"Then I behold, once more, my dear Candide," cried Pangloss.

Candide presented Martin and Cacambo to them; they embraced each other, and all spoke at once. The galley flew;

they were already in the port. Instantly Candide sent for a Jew, to whom he sold for fifty thousand sequins a diamond worth a hundred thousand, though the fellow swore to him by Abraham that he could give him no more. He immediately paid the ransom for the Baron and Pangloss. The latter threw himself at the feet of his deliverer, and bathed them with his tears; the former thanked him with a nod, and promised to return him the money on the first opportunity.

"But is it indeed possible that my sister can be in Turkey?" said he.

"Nothing is more possible," said Cacambo, "since she scours the dishes in the service of a Transylvanian prince."

Candide sent directly for two Jews and sold them some more diamonds, and then they all set out together in another galley to deliver Cunegonde from slavery.

WHAT HAPPENED TO CANDIDE, CUNEGONDE, PANGLOSS, MARTIN, ETC

"I ask your pardon once more," said Candide to the Baron, "your pardon, reverend father, for having run you through the body."

"Say no more about it," answered the Baron. "I was a little too hasty, I own, but since you wish to know by what fatality I came to be a galley-slave I will inform you. After I had been cured by the surgeon of the college of the wound you gave me, I was attacked and carried off by a party of Spanish troops, who confined me in prison at Buenos Ayres at the very time my sister was setting out thence. I asked leave to return to Rome to the General of my Order. I was appointed chaplain to the French Ambassador at Constantinople. I had not been eight days in this employment when one evening I met with a young Ichoglan, who was a very handsome fellow. The weather was warm. The young man wanted to bathe, and I took this opportunity of bathing also. I did not know that it was a capital crime for a Christian to be found naked with a young Mussulman. A cadi ordered me a hundred blows on the soles of the feet, and condemned me to the galleys. I do not think there ever was a greater act of injustice. But I should be glad to know how my sister came to be scullion to a Transylvanian prince who has taken shelter among the Turks."

"But you, my dear Pangloss," said Candide, "how can it be that I behold you again?"

"It is true," said Pangloss, "that you saw me hanged. I should have been burnt, but you may remember it rained exceedingly hard when they were going to roast me; the storm was so violent that they despaired of lighting the fire, so I was hanged because they could do no better. A surgeon purchased my body, carried me home, and dissected me. He began with making a crucial incision on me from the navel to the clavicula. One could not have been worse hanged than I was. The executioner of the Holy Inquisition was a sub-deacon, and knew how to burn people marvellously well, but he was not accustomed to hanging. The cord was wet and did not slip properly, and besides it was badly tied; in short, I still drew my breath, when the crucial incision made me give such a frightful scream that my surgeon fell flat upon his back, and imagining that he had been dissecting the devil he ran away, dying with fear, and fell down the staircase in his flight. His wife, hearing the noise, flew from the next room. She saw me stretched out upon the table with my crucial incision. She was seized with yet greater fear than her husband, fled, and tumbled over him. When they came to themselves a little, I heard the wife say to her husband: 'My dear, how could you take it into your head to dissect a heretic? Do you not know that these people always have the devil in their bodies? I will go and fetch a priest this minute to exorcise him.' At this proposal I shuddered, and mustering up what little courage I had still remaining I cried out aloud, 'Have mercy on me!' At length the Portuguese barber plucked up his spirits. He sewed up my wounds; his wife even nursed me. I was upon my legs at the end of fifteen days. The barber found me a place as lackey to a knight of Malta who was going to Venice, but finding that my master had no money to pay me my wages I entered the service of a Venetian merchant, and went with him to Constantinople. One day I took it into my head to step into a mosque, where I saw an old Iman and a very pretty young devotee who was saying her paternosters. Her bosom was uncovered, and between her breasts she had a beautiful bouquet of tulips, roses, anemones, ranunculus, hyacinths, and auriculas. She dropped her bouquet; I picked it up, and presented it to her with a profound reverence. I was so long in delivering it that the Iman began to get angry, and seeing that I was a Christian he called out for help. They carried me before the cadi, who ordered me a hundred lashes on the soles of the feet and sent me to the galleys. I was chained to the very same galley and the same bench as the young Baron. On board this galley there were four young men from Marseilles, five Neapolitan priests, and two monks from Corfu, who told us similar adventures happened daily. The Baron maintained that he had suffered greater injustice than I, and I insisted that it was far more innocent to take up a bouquet and place it again on a woman's bosom than to be found stark naked with an Ichoglan. We were continually disputing, and received twenty lashes with a bull's pizzle when the concatenation of universal events brought you to our galley, and you were good enough to ransom us."

"Well, my dear Pangloss," said Candide to him, "when you had been hanged, dissected, whipped, and were tugging at the oar, did you always think that everything happens for the best?"

"I am still of my first opinion," answered Pangloss, "for I am a philosopher and I cannot retract, especially as Leibnitz could never be wrong; and besides, the pre-established harmony is the finest thing in the world, and so is his plenum and materia subtilis."

HOW CANDIDE FOUND CUNEGONDE AND THE OLD WOMAN AGAIN

While Candide, the Baron, Pangloss, Martin, and Cacambo were relating their several adventures, were reasoning on the contingent or non-contingent events of the universe, disputing on effects and causes, on moral and physical evil, on liberty and necessity, and on the consolations a slave may feel even on a Turkish galley, they arrived at the house of the Transylvanian prince on the banks of the Propontis. The first objects which met their sight were Cunegonde and the old woman hanging towels out to dry.

The Baron paled at this sight. The tender, loving Candide, seeing his beautiful Cunegonde embrowned, with blood-shot eyes, withered neck, wrinkled cheeks, and rough, red arms, recoiled three paces, seized with horror, and then advanced out of good manners. She embraced Candide and her brother; they embraced the old woman, and Candide ransomed them both.

There was a small farm in the neighbourhood which the old woman proposed to Candide to make a shift with till the company could be provided for in a better manner. Cunegonde did not know she had grown ugly, for nobody had told her of it;

and she reminded Candide of his promise in so positive a tone that the good man durst not refuse her. He therefore intimated to the Baron that he intended marrying his sister.

"I will not suffer," said the Baron, "such meanness on her part, and such insolence on yours; I will never be reproached with this scandalous thing; my sister's children would never be able to enter the church in Germany. No; my sister shall only marry a baron of the empire."

Cunegonde flung herself at his feet, and bathed them with her tears; still he was inflexible.

"Thou foolish fellow," said Candide; "I have delivered thee out of the galleys, I have paid thy ransom, and thy sister's also; she was a scullion, and is very ugly, yet I am so condescending as to marry her; and dost thou pretend to oppose the match? I should kill thee again, were I only to consult my anger."

"Thou mayest kill me again," said the Baron, "but thou shalt not marry my sister, at least whilst I am living."

THE CONCLUSION

At the bottom of his heart Candide had no wish to marry Cunegonde. But the extreme impertinence of the Baron determined him to conclude the match, and Cunegonde pressed him so strongly that he could not go from his word. He consulted Pangloss, Martin, and the faithful Cacambo. Pangloss drew up an excellent memorial, wherein he proved that the Baron had no right over his sister, and that according to all the laws of the empire, she might marry Candide with her left hand. Martin was for throwing the Baron into the sea; Cacambo decided that it would be better to deliver him up again to the captain of the galley, after which they thought to send him back to the General Father of the Order at Rome by the first ship. This advice was well received, the old woman approved it; they said not a word to his sister; the thing was executed for a little money, and they had the double pleasure of entrapping a Jesuit, and punishing the pride of a German baron.

It is natural to imagine that after so many disasters Candide married, and living with the philosopher Pangloss, the philosopher Martin, the prudent Cacambo, and the old woman, having besides brought so many diamonds from the country of the ancient Incas, must have led a very happy life. But he was so much imposed upon by the Jews that he had nothing left except his small farm; his wife became uglier every day, more peevish and unsupportable; the old woman was infirm and even more fretful than Cunegonde. Cacambo, who worked in the garden, and took vegetables for sale to Constantinople, was fatigued with hard work, and cursed his destiny. Pangloss was in despair at not shining in some German university. For Martin, he was firmly persuaded that he would be as badly off elsewhere, and therefore bore things patiently. Candide, Martin, and Pangloss sometimes disputed about morals and metaphysics. They often saw passing under the windows of their farm boats full of Effendis, Pashas, and Cadis, who were going into banishment to Lemnos, Mitylene, or Erzeroum. And they saw other Cadis, Pashas, and Effendis coming to supply the place of the exiles, and afterwards exiled in their turn. They saw heads decently impaled for presentation to the Sublime Porte. Such spectacles as these increased the number of their dissertations; and when they did not dispute time hung so heavily upon their hands, that one day the old woman ventured to say to them:

"I want to know which is worse, to be ravished a hundred times by negro pirates, to have a buttock cut off, to run the gauntlet among the Bulgarians, to be whipped and hanged at an auto-da-fé, to be dissected, to row in the galleys—in short, to go through all the miseries we have undergone, or to stay here and have nothing to do?"

"It is a great question," said Candide.

This discourse gave rise to new reflections, and Martin especially concluded that man was born to live either in a state of distracting inquietude or of lethargic disgust. Candide did not quite agree to that, but he affirmed nothing. Pangloss owned that he had always suffered horribly, but as he had once asserted that everything went wonderfully well, he asserted it still, though he no longer believed it.

What helped to confirm Martin in his detestable principles, to stagger Candide more than ever, and to puzzle Pangloss, was that one day they saw Paquette and Friar Giroflée land at the farm in extreme misery. They had soon squandered their three thousand piastres, parted, were reconciled, quarrelled again, were thrown into gaol, had escaped, and Friar Giroflée had at length become Turk. Paquette continued her trade wherever she went, but made nothing of it.

"I foresaw," said Martin to Candide, "that your presents would soon be dissipated, and only make them the more miserable. You have rolled in millions of money, you and Cacambo; and yet you are not happier than Friar Giroflée and Paquette."

"Ha!" said Pangloss to Paquette, "Providence has then brought you amongst us again, my poor child! Do you know that you cost me the tip of my nose, an eye, and an ear, as you may see? What a world is this!"

And now this new adventure set them philosophising more than ever.

In the neighbourhood there lived a very famous Dervish who was esteemed the best philosopher in all Turkey, and they went to consult him. Pangloss was the speaker.

"Master," said he, "we come to beg you to tell why so strange an animal as man was made."

"With what meddlest thou?" said the Dervish; "is it thy business?"

"But, reverend father," said Candide, "there is horrible evil in this world."

"What signifies it," said the Dervish, "whether there be evil or good? When his highness sends a ship to Egypt, does he trouble his head whether the mice on board are at their ease or not?"

"What, then, must we do?" said Pangloss.

"Hold your tongue," answered the Dervish.

"I was in hopes," said Pangloss, "that I should reason with you a little about causes and effects, about the best of possible worlds, the origin of evil, the nature of the soul, and the pre-established harmony."

At these words, the Dervish shut the door in their faces.

During this conversation, the news was spread that two Viziers and the Mufti had been strangled at Constantinople, and that several of their friends had been impaled. This catastrophe made a great noise for some hours. Pangloss, Candide, and Martin, returning to the little farm, saw a good old man taking the fresh air at his door under an orange bower. Pangloss, who was as inquisitive as he was argumentative, asked the old man what was the name of the strangled Mufti.

"I do not know," answered the worthy man, "and I have not known the name of any Mufti, nor of any Vizier. I am entirely ignorant of the event you mention; I presume in general that they who meddle with the administration of public affairs die sometimes miserably, and that they deserve it; but I never trouble my head about what is transacting at Constantinople; I content myself with sending there for sale the fruits of the garden which I cultivate."

Having said these words, he invited the strangers into his house; his two sons and two daughters presented them with several sorts of sherbet, which they made themselves, with Kaimak enriched with the candied-peel of citrons, with oranges, lemons, pine-apples, pistachio-nuts, and Mocha coffee unadulterated with the bad coffee of Batavia or the American islands. After which the two daughters of the honest Mussulman perfumed the strangers' beards.

"You must have a vast and magnificent estate," said Candide to the Turk.

"I have only twenty acres," replied the old man; "I and my children cultivate them; our labour preserves us from three great evils—weariness, vice, and want."

Candide, on his way home, made profound reflections on the old man's conversation.

"This honest Turk," said he to Pangloss and Martin, "seems to be in a situation far preferable to that of the six kings with whom we had the honour of supping."

"Grandeur," said Pangloss, "is extremely dangerous according to the testimony of philosophers. For, in short, Eglon, King of Moab, was assassinated by Ehud; Absalom was hung by his hair, and pierced with three darts; King Nadab, the son of Jeroboam, was killed by Baasa; King Ela by Zimri; Ahaziah by Jehu; Athaliah by Jehoiada; the Kings Jehoiakim, Jeconiah, and Zedekiah, were led into captivity. You know how perished Croesus, Astyages, Darius, Dionysius of Syracuse, Pyrrhus, Perscus, Hannibal, Jugurtha, Ariovistus, Cæsar, Pompey, Nero, Otho, Vitellius, Domitian, Richard II. of England, Edward II., Henry VI., Richard III., Mary Stuart, Charles I., the three Henrys of France, the Emperor Henry IV.! You know——"

"I know also," said Candide, "that we must cultivate our garden."

"You are right," said Pangloss, "for when man was first placed in the Garden of Eden, he was put there *ut operaretur eum,* that he might cultivate it; which shows that man was not born to be idle."

"Let us work," said Martin, "without disputing; it is the only way to render life tolerable."

The whole little society entered into this laudable design, according to their different abilities. Their little plot of land produced plentiful crops. Cunegonde was, indeed, very ugly, but she became an excellent pastry cook; Paquette worked at embroidery; the old woman looked after the linen. They were all, not excepting Friar Giroflée, of some service or other; for he made a good joiner, and became a very honest man.

Pangloss sometimes said to Candide:

"There is a concatenation of events in this best of all possible worlds: for if you had not been kicked out of a magnificent castle for love of Miss Cunegonde: if you had not been put into the Inquisition: if you had not walked over America: if you had not stabbed the Baron: if you had not lost all your sheep from the fine country of El Dorado: you would not be here eating preserved citrons and pistachio-nuts."

"All that is very well," answered Candide, "but let us cultivate our garden."

Publisher's Note

This book was produced as part of the Publishing master's degree program at Western Colorado University, Graduate Program in Creative Writing. The students worked cooperatively to produce these fine new editions of worthy public-domain works. The intent is to bring literary classics to a new readership. For the enjoyment of a modern audience, some minor revisions to archaic terms or punctuation may have been made.

Because these works were written in a different time, some attitudes and phrasing may seem outdated to a modern audience. After careful consideration, rather than revising the author's work, we have chosen to preserve the original wording and intent.

About the Author

Voltaire, pen name for Parisian Enlightenment writer Francois-Marie Arouet (1694-1778), was a prolific writer and critic of the church, royalty, and government. Well-versed in philosophy and history, he used satire and humor to critique hypocrisy with a scathing wit and thinly veiled allusions to political and philosophical figures. No stranger to scandal, Arouet adopted the pen name Voltaire after an eleven-month stint in the Bastille. He mingled with high society, royalty, and natural philosophers across Europe, and was an intellectual celebrity of his time.

Of note was his support for the theories of Isaac Newton, which author and Voltaire scholar Adam Roberts speaks to this in the foreword to this publication, *A Voltaire Triptych*. Voltaire's masterwork, Candide, has inspired many writers to this day, including Kevin J. Anderson and Neal Peart's novel *Clockwork Angels*, published by WordFire Press.

About the Foreword Author

Adam Roberts is a British writer, critic and scholar. As a prolific science fiction, fantasy, parody, and literary criticism author, his work has been nominated for and won many awards, including the Arthur C. Clarke award, The British Science Fiction Association award, and the John W. Campbell award. In 2018, he was elected vice-president of the H.G. Wells Society. As a Professor in Nineteenth-century Literature and Culture at Royal Holloway, University of London, he teaches English literature and Creative Writing.

About the Editor

Carrie Christopher is a multi-creative Colorado-based artist working in words, sounds, images, and objects. She shares her deep appreciation for the absurd, the rebellious, and the transformative magic of nature and liminal spaces through her art, writing, and field recordings that are available at CarrieChristopher-Creative.com.

When not creating, slush-pile reading for Baen Books, or spending time with her two rescue cats, Carrie is a publishing intern at WordFire Press. She aims to earn her M.A. in Publishing through the Western Colorado University Graduate Program in Creative Writing in July 2026, then start her own indie press.

Carrie's publishing credits include editor of *A Voltaire Triptych* and editorial team member for *The Deep Dark Woods Anthology*, both due for release in summer 2026, and proofreader for Frank Herbert's *Soul Catcher* re-issue, all published through WordFire Press.

Her debut speculative fiction novel, *Quicksand Bardo*, is due for release in 2027.

WordFire Classics

Mother of Frankenstein: Maria: or, The Wrongs of Woman &
Memoirs of the Author of A Vindication of the Rights of Woman
by Mary Wollstonecraft

We: The 100th Anniversary Edition
by Yevgeny Zamyatin

One Stormy Night : A Story Challenge That Created the Gothic
Horror Genre
by Lord Byron, Dr. John William Polidori, and Mary Shelley

HOLIDAY CLASSICS

The Ghost of Christmas Always
by Charles Dickens & Kevin J. Anderson

The Santa Claus Stories
by L. Frank Baum

Our list of other WordFire Press authors and titles is always
growing. To find out more and to shop our selection of titles,
visit us at:
wordfirepress.com

facebook.com/WordfireIncWordfirePress
x.com/WordFirePress
instagram.com/WordFirePress
bookbub.com/profile/41097845 12

www.ingramcontent.com/pod-product-compliance
Lightning Source LLC
Chambersburg PA
CBHW061423160726
47995CB00003B/732